IRISH LAHCHYNA

© *2015*

Published by Royalty Publishing House
www.royaltypublishinghouse.com

ACKNOWLEDGEMENTS

First, I want to give an honor to my lord and savior for giving me the strength to write this book and blessing my family and me every day. To my kids Isaiah, Ifamion "Malik" and Iaiyana, y'all give me the reason to strive for better and give me purpose in life. I love y'all for life.

To Jermaine, thanks for helping get through some though spots and helping me keep focus. To my mom Sharon "Peach Passion" thanks for everything and all the arguments telling me I got this, love ya. To my DAD Isaac "P-We" and mom Alice I love y'all both. To my sisters and brothers, Me-Me, Kayrese, Courtney, Nikki, Tequila, Donald, Dennis, Daron and Jerzy I love y'all more than words can express.

To My Ace boon coon, my ride or die chick Cassandra "Keyla" Haywood I love you girl. I told you trouble don't last always I got you boo. Times get hard and we seem to get lost in other situations but we always got each other back. Loyalty is a strong thing but what we have is stronger.

To my Weeks, James, Robertson, Carter, Benton, and Williams family thanks for all the laughs, hugs and tears I appreciate it. To Bertha Mae thanks lady for just being there and never question what I needed. To Ms. Laese Clark thank you I can never repay for all you have done for me thank you. One day I hope I can do as much for you as you do for others.

Last but not least, Francisco "Frankie" thanks for your prayers for me and my family. You keep telling everything is going to be alright and GOD got me. Thanks for everything.

To Ms. Porscha "Trap Queen" Sterling and the Royalty Family, thank you for reading my work and giving me a chance to share my book to the world. I love being a part of such amazing team. This is just the beginning of something I pray that that will last a lifetime.

Diggin' Your Vibe

Vibe

A Hood Romance

A Novel By

Irish Lahchyna

Remember....
You haven't read 'til you've read
#Royalty
Check us out at
www.royaltypublishinghouse.com
Royalty drops #dopebooks

If you would like to join our team,
submit the first 3 -4 chapters of
your completed manuscript to
submissions@royaltypublishinghouse.com

IRISH LAHCHYNA

LYANA

"Oh, hell nah, I know I don't see what my eyes are seeing!" Tasi yelled across the room.

I looked in the direction she was screaming about. We were in the middle of Crabtree Mall in Raleigh, and all eyes were on her as she made a scene. I love my girl but she was has as hood as it comes sometimes. Tasi and I have been friends since middle school, best friends at that. She was more like a sister than a friend.

We rocked harder than most and we truly valued our friendship. Tasi has always been a big chick, but by far, the prettiest. She held her weight perfectly. At twenty-one years old, 250 pounds, five-feet-five, brown skin, big butt and 34D breasts, my chick rocked. She could pull more men and women than most. Yes, my chick is bisexual and very outspoken. If you thought big girl jokes were going to make her feel embarrassed, you were gladly mistaken. She put people that did big girl jokes, to shame, and that's why I loved her.

"Lyana, you heard that shit she said to me?"

I just looked and said, "So what." She was referring to Mex and Cha walking into Journeys. Mex has been my crush since forever, but we never spoke and I've never approached him, so whatever. Don't get me wrong, your girl Lyana Duhtrum was blessed, mixed with black and Cuban. I'm twenty-two, five-feet-four, 200 pounds, with hair to the middle of my back, light brown eyes and ass for days, with a flat stomach and 36C breasts. Yes, I was blessed by the gods. "I don't care about that," I said in my country Wayne voice.

"Tasi, let's go, I have to study for my midterms and you're making a scene." We headed to my 2015 Suburban; I love big trucks or SUVS. We got in and headed home.

MEX

I was in Journeys with Cha when I heard Tasi holler something, but I paid it no mind. I knew her and Lyana were together. I had to peep at Lyana because she was bad; I mean she had me drooling from afar. I'm Mexquan Salvador, Mex for short. I was well known in the streets because my mother and father, Sambo and Stella Salvador, are royal drug dealers in North Carolina. Everyone knew who they were, and I was not to be fucked with, but really, I wanted no parts of the drug empire. I wanted to be different, but as a son of a kingpin that was hard to do. I just wanted to be normal. However, born in this lifestyle, there was nothing normal about it.

I was with Cha, a girl from around the way. Chayalesa was everyone's jump off, but I promised her a trip to the mall because she had a bomb head game and I like to keep my promises. I just hope she doesn't think anything else, because I was deading that shit ASAP. I'm a handsome, young black man, twenty-five years old, with no criminal record. I stand at six-feet-three, 220 pounds, all muscle, with forty tattoos; I love art you could say. I was ready to go and Cha was getting on my last nerve. I hope no one thinks we're together because that was far from the truth. I don't cuff hood rats.

I yelled at Cha, "Let's go," because she was annoying as hell and I was getting tired of looking at her. I only spent $500 on her and she really thought she was doing something. *Silly girl*, I thought. She looked up and nodded her okay, and I proceeded to walk her to her 2000 Ford Mustang. There was no way she was getting in my whip, hell nah. I left her at her car, headed to my 2015 Bugatti, jumped in and went back to Charlotte where I belonged.

LYANA

On the ride back to Charlotte, Tasi and I were listing to Nicki and Queen B's "Feeling Myself."

"Feeling myself, feeling myself, I'm feeling my, feeling myself."

We were singing along because we really were feeling ourselves. I could not wait to get home because tonight, my girl and I were going to turn up. A bitch was almost finished with college and I needed to relieve some stress. I was beyond stressed. School was tiring as hell, but I wanted to finish, to prove I could do something without my parents' help. I wanted to be a Physician Assistant and in June, that's what I will be, Dr. Lyana Duhtrum.

We were going to some club called Fast Forward. It was the club's grand opening tonight, and I was more than happy to get out and hopefully, get some head. A bitch was experiencing a drought. I mean, my shit was dry as hell. The damn desert might look at me and laugh. I wasn't a hoe or a virgin, but a little licky isn't going to hurt nobody. My last relationship was five years ago with Desmond, and he broke my heart to the core; so much so, that I didn't want another relationship.

"Tasi, girl, Desmond is going to want to marry me after tonight cause I'm going to put it on him," I told Tasi on the phone. I was getting my bags ready because I was going on the east end to Desmond's house for the weekend. It was Thursday and I had no plans for Friday, so I decided to surprise him a day early. I jumped in my '99 Durango and headed to his house for a night to remember, or so I thought.

I got to the house, cut off my engine and made sure my lip-gloss was popping before heading in. I used my key to enter the house. I knew he was there because his Porsche was in the driveway. I didn't say anything because I wanted to surprise him. Heading up stairs to his master suite, I heard moaning. I was hoping he was watching a flick, but to my surprise, Desmond was pumping his next door neighbor, Mr. Rick. I made my presence known when I screamed "YOU NASTY DICK NIGGA!" and left.

Right then, I made up my mind not to trust dudes anymore, but I was like a dog in heat and I needed to relive some pressure tonight.

MEX

I was happy as hell to get back to the 'lotte. Cha was getting on my damn nerves with her damn mouth. I headed to the block to chop it up with my boys. Tony, Los, Bug, and Marcus, they were my day ones. I love them like brothers because I have none. If you were to look up the definition of loyalty, I'm pretty sure their names would be there. Tony "Tone" Garris Jr. is my right hand. We've been through so much it's crazy. My dad, Sambo and his dad, Tony "Killer" Garris, are best friends. They ran my family empire because they *were* family.

"Mex, what the hell are you doing with Cha in the mall?" Tony asked.

"Man, how the hell you know that shit?"

"Because nigga, you stupid as fuck, that's why your crazy ass ain't gone ever learn. Nigga, your dick is going to fall off messing with dirty butts." My crew started laughing at me, but it was all good though.

"Whatever man, how yawls know I was with her thot ass anyway?" I questioned.

"Because she posted that shit on the book saying *'With my man out shopping'* and she had a nerve to have kiss emojis," Los told me and showed me that shit on his phone. Heated was not even a word for me right now. I was boiling hot. Seriously, I wanted to put some lead in Cha's ass.

"Whateva, niggas, I'm out, heading to the crib."

"Hold up, hold up," Tony said. "Now I know your ass going out with us tonight man, we going to that new spot downtown."

"Damn, I ain't got anything to wear out tonight. Why yawl didn't tell me earlier, I would have copped something from the mall?" I asked.

"See nigga, I knew you were with that thot, and your ass got plenty of clothes, you pretty boy Floyd ass muthafucka," Los replied.

"Alright man, I'm down I will be at the spot around nine and Bug, your ass better be on time because I ain't waiting on your ass all night nigga," I laughed.

"Okay, I will be ready Mex, damn, yawl always picking on me," Bug said. We all started laughing before departing ways.

TASI

I was more than happy to go out tonight, I needed to let loose a little bit. Working with kids all day at my mother's daycare, had a chick beyond tired. I loved helping my mom because I loved kids, but I didn't want any; at least not now, anyway. I got a spot in Big Topps Modeling Agency and I was ready to celebrate with my bestie on both of our success. Yes, Shantasia "Tasi" Weldon is big and beautiful. I loved my size! Other chicks my size would either be depressed because of their weight or just give up on life. That was not me. I loved me and no one could be me, not even if he or she tried.

I got out of the shower and applied lotion to my body, while sitting on my king size bed, when I heard my phone going off. I picked it up and noticed I had five messages. There were three from Tony and two from Star. They were going to be the death of me. I wasn't in a relationship because I was chasing the money, but I was full of energy so I gave them the business. Tony was a chocolate, sexy nigga, dreads past his ass, stood at six-feet-two, 220 pounds with the body of a god. Yes, a bitch liked them dark and lovely; the blacker the berry, the sweeter… you know. Star is a pretty ole blackberry standing at five-feet-seven, 150 pounds, 44DD breasts, with an ass that made your eyes pop out and titties every newborn would want to suck. I had them both sprung. I might be big, but I had men and women so whipped, my bank account was looking like I made six figures. Yes, my pussy was a lethal weapon and my tongue had women leaving their husbands and kids.

Tonight was about Lyana and I. We are going to have a ball and I cannot wait. I want to look sexy tonight, so I put on my Expression jumper by Qristyl Frazier and my six-inch Chanel pumps. I was ready to roll, hoping I'd see Tony tonight. I know him and his crew are going to be in the place. He is one of Mex's boys, my bestie's crush since like forever. So, tonight if all goes according to plan, I will have Tony and get Lyana some wood in the process, though I know that she doesn't want any. Regardless of her past,

Lyana needs to understand that not every man is like Desmond, and I hope that tonight she gets that understanding.

The club was packed and I don't do lines, so I hooked the bouncer up with two hundred to let us in V.I.P. It was well worth is because as soon we got in, all eyes were on us. Lyana had on a see-through Michael Kors dress and black stilettos, with her hair parted down the middle, letting it hang over her shoulders and down her back. My girl is bad! We got to the V.I.P section and I was in awe. It was designed in red, black and white, with a tint of purple. It was gorgeous and the colors fit perfectly. The waiter came up and we both ordered *Sex on the Beach*. We were in the club having fun, when I looked to my left and spotted my targets, Mex and Tony with their crew. I bumped Lyana.

"Come on let's go speak to Mex and them," I said.

Lyana blew out a sigh and was like, "no Tasi, you know I get nervous around Mex. Even though he's been my crush since middle school, I can't be around him."

"I don't understand, you've had this crush since like forever and haven't said one damn thing to this man. Well, tonight that's going to be a wrap 'cause you're going with me over there," I stated. I grabbed Lyana's hand and we were headed to talk to Mex and Tony.

MEX

We were having a ball in the club, chilling and drinking. Los and Bug smoked weed but the rest of us just drank; that was not our thing. We were singing Future's "Fuck up Some Commas."

"Let's fuck up some commas. Fuck up some commas yea, forty thou to a hundred thou, a hundred thou 'nother hundred thou, three hundred thou to five hundred thou, a million y'all that's how my money shower."

I was feeling the music until Tony bumped me and told me to look to my right. I saw Lyana and Tasi coming toward us. Lyana was looking bad as fuck with that see-through dress and underneath was a Pink by Victoria's Secret lingerie set. I had to step to her tonight because the way she was looking, I saw the men in club wanting her on a platter and that wasn't going to happen. She was going to be mine after tonight.

"What's up Tasi, what's going on girl? I know your ass over here for Tone's skinny ass," I laughed.

Tasi was a big chick, but I loved her like a sister. Her ass was about her business, and even with her weight, no one could really fuck with her. I was praying Los' ass was going to keep his mouth shut, because he was drunk and high and didn't know how to control his tongue when he got at that stage sometimes. But, him and Tasi going at it was nothing new. They always went at it. Being around them two would have you crying at the jokes they had on each other.

I turned to Lyana and said, "What's up love, you looking hella sexy tonight. Who are you trying to take home?" She was smiling hard and that made her ass even sexier. I was starting to feel butterflies fluttering in my stomach, and that was a feeling I've never felt before. "So who are you trying to take home?" I asked her again.

Lyana turned to me and said, "No one, I came to celebrate a little and enjoy myself."

"What are you celebrating, Lyana?" She told me she was graduating from PA school and I was amazed because girls around this neck of the woods, were not about that life. Knowing her and Tasi were doing something positive with their lives, made me have the utmost respect for them. They did not allow themselves to become a product of the hood.

"Damn baby girl, I admire you for that. Since you're celebrating, can a nigga take you out to eat after the club, my treat?" I asked her.

She gave me a sexy ass look and said, "Yeah, you can take me out."

TONY

Tasi was looking good as fuck in that dress, and I can't lie, I was feeling baby girl hard as hell. I liked my girls big and thick, and Tasi was the girl I wanted. I mean, she had a nigga ready to wife her ass, but she was not hearing that shit. She was on her grown woman status and I couldn't do anything but respect that. She was about that money and that shit made me love her more. I knew baby girl was bisexual and every man's dream was two women in the bed with them, but I was a selfish nigga, I didn't want to share. She was enough for me and she was going to be all mine.

"Tasi, you know you're coming home with me right, and don't try to front. You out here with that dress on, I hope you wasn't plan on taking that shit back because once we get to the spot that shit is going to be in shreds." I wasn't playing, I was going to rip that shit right off her ass. Looking that good should be a sin, and I didn't like the way the men was looking at my baby.

"Okay Tony, I'm coming home with you," she said, "but you know I got to tell Lyana because we rode together."

I heard Los say behind me, "Tony, I know your ass ain't talking to that big ass bowl over there." I knew it was about to be on because Los and Tasi always got into it, but it was nothing but love though. They could crack jokes on each other one minute and hug the next. But no one else better not have tried that shit, because Tasi's mouth was the truth, and if you thought you had a big girl joke, you'd better go hard or go home. If you didn't, she would make your ass cry and embarrass your ass, making you feel like a kid that got a whooping for stealing.

"Whatever nigga, you Garfield, lasagna eating, look alike ass muthafucka," Tasi screamed at Los. Los was at a loss for words. The whole V.I.P fell out laughing.

"You got that one, Tasi," Los said.

"Enough of that, you ready to head out with me, baby girl, or what?" I asked her.

"Let's wait until the club ends. Let's just enjoy the moment for a little while," Tasi said. I really didn't want to wait, but I knew she was worth every minute.

LYANA

The club was closing and I couldn't wait to get into Mex's Bugatti. That shit was sexy and I knew it drove to perfection. I was so nervous that I knew I going was going to say something stupid. Mex was holding my hand as we made it to his car.

"Mex, you know I drove here, right?"

"I know. Tasi is driving your car to Tone's house and we will pick it up later. Get in Lyana."

"Where are we going?" I asked.

"Just sit back and enjoy the ride, baby." Mex calling me baby had my panties so drenched I had to pull my legs together. We drove for like an hour and ended up at a house in front of the beach.

"Where are we?" I asked. The place was beautiful on the outside but when we got inside, it was like a house off of MTV cribs. Mex led me to the kitchen's candle lit table. There were crab legs, lobster, oysters, broccoli and cheese, corn on the cob, sweet rolls and white wine. I was so amazed at the lengths he went to for this dinner. If he was trying to make a first impression, he got an 'A' because this was awesome.

We finished eating, went into the living room, and lay in front of the fireplace. We spent some time getting to know each other. Mex told me he had been watching me for a while, causing me to blushing from ear to ear. If he only knew how much I had a crush on him. He told me he had a sister named Keshena and she was sixteen. That was a shock because I thought he was the only child, but that was good to know. At least her name wasn't in the streets. He told me he knew the ins and outs of his family drug empire, but doesn't want any parts of it. It was so ironic because my dad was in the drug game and I wanted no parts of it either, but I didn't want to reveal that to him. I told him I knew a lot about the drug game myself; he looked at me funny but blew it off.

The wine was taking affect; I was feeling nice and wanted some head, but I didn't want Mex to think I was a hoe or anything. Mex asked me was I ready to go, but I really didn't want this night to end. I was finally in the same room with a man I wanted for so long. I asked him could we stay the night, and he had the biggest smile ever. He told me the guest bedroom was down the hall to the right. He helped me up from the floor so I could take care of my hygiene. As soon as he helped me up, our eyes met. He kissed me with so much passion it was like love at first sight. He picked me up bridal style and took me to a room; I'm guessing it was the master suite. There was a king size bed decorated in white and gold, in addition to the room's interior being draped in white and gold. He stripped me out of my dress and I stripped him out of his wife beater, True Religion jeans and Calvin Klein boxers.

Still kissing, we entered the shower lathering each other with soap. I was so horny I really did not care. All I wanted was for him to be inside of me. He began to kiss me on my neck and then started sucking on my nipples from right to left. I was in heaven and loving every bit of it. He kissed me until he got to my freshly shaven pussy. He lifted me up above his head and feast on my kitty like it was his last meal on earth. I was screaming his name then he asked me the golden question, was it his, and I said yes, yes, yes, as if we were getting married tomorrow. He said "cum for your man, baby." As I did, he licked up my sweet juices, before putting me down and heading to the bed.

MEX

Lyana had brought the beast out of your boy. Never in all of my years of fucking chicks, have I ever gone to these lengths, but I was feeling shorty something terrible. As I laid her on the bed, I admired her body; she was gorgeous and I could see me cuffing her ass. I hope she knew once I put this pipe on her it was a wrap, because she belonged to me. She began to massage my eleven inches and put it in her mouth. She was slurping on my shit sloppily as hell. She really didn't know what she was doing and I was going teach her; however, not tonight, I wanted that pussy. I laid her back and opened her legs to get to her opening. I put all eleven inches in her. She was so tight I had to go slow and work my way in. Once I got in, I wanted to explode. I wasn't going to give her the satisfaction of calling me a minute man, so I held back. I dicked her down in all type of positions, but when I got her in my favorite position, the hand that rocked the cradle, we both exploded.

As I took a deep breath, I realized I didn't have a condom on. What the hell was I thinking? I laid shorty down on the bed. I had dicked her down so good, she was out for the count. I went into the bathroom to handle my hygiene then got Lyana a washcloth and cleaned her up. I know we just fucked, but I hope in the morning, Lyana realizes she is no longer single. In addition, we were going to the drug store to get a plan B pill, because I didn't if she was on both control or not.

SAMBO

I was heading to the gym to work out, when I got a call from my connect in Cali informing me that my shipment was coming in earlier than I thought. I have been waiting for this shipment for a while; two-hundred bricks of pure uncut cocaine and one-hundred pounds of weed. I wanted to take over Virginia and Georgia, wanting my empire to spread beyond North Carolina. I wanted Mex to get on board with the family business, but he really didn't want any parts of this life. Even if he didn't want this lifestyle, he was going to get it any way. Being my next heir, he really didn't have a choice in the matter. I continued to show him the ins and outs of the drug game. He needed to know this lifestyle isn't fair and you always had to watch your back.

My wife, Stella is my ride or die chick. She rides for me in every way and I love her unconditionally. Now, my baby girl was spoiled rotten and had me wrapped around her finger. Whatever she wanted, she got it from Daddy. She was sixteen going on thirty. She never went out or hung with a crowd, staying to herself and not getting into any trouble. She was her daddy's baby and her mother's princess. My baby was lethal with a gun. She is a sharp shooter and can kill with her bare hands. Her, Tony and Mex were trained by the best, me, Tony and Stella. We wanted our kids to be silent but deadly if needed to be, because the streets were ruthless and you never knew when you needed to be prepared.

I called my ace, my bro, Tony, known as Killer in the streets. Our names rang bells in the 'lotte. "Yo Killer, that package is being shipped early so we have to make a trip to Cali in two days. I want the boys ready, and make sure our spots and stashes are switched to the new location."

"Alright, I'll call Tone now to let him and the boys know what the deal is. Be safe bro, hit me up later," Tony replied. My God son, Tone was in the game and he loved it. I mean, my son's whole crew was in the family, but my son wasn't game, and I could not stand that fact alone. Once I finished my workout, I was headed home to my wife and daughter. I called but Mex he didn't pick up, so I sent him a text to let him know to meet me at the house. I stayed on the South side of the 'lotte. Yeah, I got money out the ass but I'm a hood nigga, and I stayed among what I knew. I had a nice setup. My house consisted of ten bedrooms with their own full bathrooms, a kitchen, huge living and dining room, pool, theater room, Jacuzzi, basketball court and huge patio. I had a man cave I just added to the house and loved it; it provided safety and relaxation. I decorated it in blue and white, my favorite colors.

I walked into the house, where my wife greeted me with a kiss and told me dinner would be ready by six. I went to my man cave and chilled for a bit, thinking how I was about to tell my son he had to join me on this trip because he was going to help me take over Virginia and Georgia.

LYANA

I woke up the next morning feeling hella good, but I forgot where the hell I was at. I heard singing coming from somewhere and I followed the sound. I end up in the kitchen, where Mex was standing in his boxers cooking breakfast. I had to think to myself *so that wasn't a dream, I had sex with Mex*. Just then, he turned around and spoke to me.

"Good morning beautiful, how are you this morning?" I was happy Mex didn't know what he was doing to my pussy right now. I had just noticed I was wrapped in a sheet.

"Lyana, you know you are no longer single, right?" he asked me.

I said "yes" as all the memories from last night came flooding back to my brain. I was Mex's girl and always wanted to be that, but little did he know I was still going to be me. I know Mex had money, but I was an independent chick who loved to make my own.

"Lyana, are you on some form of birth control?" he asked unexpectedly.

"No, why did you ask me that question Mex?" I replied, puzzled.

"Because Lyana, when we had sex last night we used no protection whatsoever, so we need to do something." I started to panic. Oh my God, this nigga had random hood rats he was sleeping with and he went in me raw dog. I wasn't feeling this shit at all.

"Mex, let's go to the pharmacy right now. I don't want any breakfast. Let's go now, please. Where the hell is my clothes, Mex?" As I made my way back to the room, I saw my dress and underwear on the floor, torn up. Now what was I going to wear?

"L, I got you, I went and picked up an outfit for you this morning from Wal-Mart. I know this isn't your type of wear, but it was the only thing open at that time of morning."

"So, if you figured that out, why the hell didn't you get me the plan B pill?"

"I did L, it's in the bathroom under the sink," Mex replied with a smirk. I was still mad even if he did think of all the right things. I jumped into the shower, put on a white t-shirt and a pair of gray joggers. Once I finished getting dressed, I grabbed my iPhone 6 off the nightstand, powered it on and headed for the kitchen to get some water to take this pill. My phone started to go off. I had six messages from my dad, two from my mom, and three from Tasi. I called Tasi first to see what she wanted.

"Hey chicka, what's up with you?" she asked me. "I see your car is still in Tone's yard so that must mean you're still with Mex. You nasty heifer, tell all, and I do mean tell all, 'cause I want to know every last detail."

I had to laugh because that girl was crazy, but I just told her I'd be there in a little while and hung up. The text from my dad and mom stated they wanted me to call; they were worried about me. I called my Dad he picked up on the first ring.

"Lyana, I need you to come to the house in the next hour." My dad sounded mad and I didn't know what that was about, but I was about to do something I've never done and that was to be late when he requested my presence. I looked for Mex and he was in the living room watching basketball on his 70-inch TV. He looked up at me and asked me was I ready to go or were we going to talk about us.

CAPPO

My daughter, Lyana was getting ahead of herself more than she knew. I had eyes everywhere and I just found out my daughter was with Mex. The thought of my daughter fucking around with my competition's son, had me angry has hell. I try to keep the streets from my home but I was a street nigga, the streets choose me. I wasn't always like this. I grew up in a two-parent household along with three siblings, two sisters and one brother. I graduated with honors, was at the top of my class, and went to Spellman College to study law. Both of my parents were lawyers so it was only right for me to follow their lead. Since I was the baby, they expected that of me. My siblings were older and all had already followed another path in life.

Spellman was where my life changed. I met Tanya Stalls, the love of my life. I could truly say we were in love. My sophomore year and her senior year in college, Tonya got pregnant. I now had a family to take care of. I was so used to being spoiled by my parents that I thought they would be happy for me, but I was so wrong. My father did help us with a place, but that was it. They said they were disappointed in me and told me I needed to man up and take care of my family.

Tanya graduated, pregnant and all. I was so proud of my baby. She got a job at a law firm making good money. I dropped out of school because I was presented with a job, which was needed in order to take care of my family. Sambo gave me a chance with his crew and I loved every minute of it. I was bringing in more money than I could count. It helped my family in an amazing way. Everyone knew who I was in the streets. Tony gave me my own crew to run; they were like family to me. Being the man that I was, I could not let my girl make more money than me, so it was mandatory I paid all the bills and Tanya just stacked her money... well, both of our money in the bank. Since I had money and Tanya had money, we moved to a nice home on the East side of town, but I was still a hood nigga at heart, I just wanted better for my family.

I flew my girl out to Vegas and we got married when she was eight months pregnant with Lyana. On the way back home, Tanya's water broke. Ten hours later, my baby was born at 9lbs. 10oz. My baby was perfect, mixed with black and Cuban. I knew I had to keep my eye on my love bug. Tanya was full-blooded Cuban, with both parents descending from Cuba. I got along with them perfectly.

After Tanya had the baby, the baby weight had her thick as hell. She was already thick, but that baby weight made her extra sexy. A woman about her money, with a banging body is every man's dream; all men desired to have a woman like that by his side. My baby took care of home and after her six weeks, she went right back to work. I couldn't stop her hustle though, that was her determination. One day I was making a run for Sambo on the West side. My phone started ringing and in the background, I heard my wife moaning on the phone, having sex with someone. I could not believe my ears.

As I began to listen, I could hear my baby pleading to Sambo she didn't want to do this because she loved me and he was married to Stella. Hearing my love like that drove me insane. I was two hours away and I had to pull over to compose myself because at that present time, all I saw was death and Sambo was going to feel my pain. I turned around and headed to the house to go get my wife. I pushed one-hundred miles per hour trying to get to her as quickly as possible. As I pulled up to the house, I pulled out my two desert eagles, ready for war. My mind was going in all different directions and I really couldn't refrain myself from what was about to happen to that fuck nigga, Sambo. How could you betray family like that? I never knew hurt like that before. I loved that nigga like no other, and for him to hurt me like that made me trust no nigga. I was done with him, no more. When I was young, I heard don't ever bite the hand that feeds you, but in this case I wasn't going to bite, I was going to kill that nigga.

I went into the house like a mad man, yelling Tanya's name. I got no response, so I started to panic. As I got to my bathroom, I heard the shower running. I went in with my desert eagles pointed because I didn't know what I might see. I saw my baby balled up in a fetal position in the shower, crying her eyes out. I got in the shower with her, not caring that I was getting wet. All I wanted to do was hold my wife in my arms. I carried her bridal style to the room. I could see the hurt in her eyes and I began to cry with her.

"I promise you baby, that nigga going to suffer bae, he is going to suffer a horrible death."

She looked up to me and said, "Baby, I know you want to kill him, but don't do it baby, he ain't worth the bullet." I looked at her as if she was crazy.

"What are you saying, Tanya, you got feelings for this nigga or something?" All I saw was red. I laid her on the bed and was about to head out the door. I couldn't believe the shit that just came out my wife's mouth, like she was feeling the nigga that raped her or something. Tanya yelled my name but I didn't want to talk, because I was feeling some kind of fucked up at the moment. I was about to leave when Tanya got up running behind me, jumping on my back, yelling and screaming.

"I told you I didn't want you in this lifestyle, look what it has caused me, heartache and pain, Cappo!" I couldn't take looking at her like that. I got in my car and peeled off. First stop, Sambo, he was about to meet his maker.

I parked five blocks from Sambo's crib. He must have known I was coming because that nigga upped his security by fifty men. I couldn't get to him like I wanted to because one man with over 50 guards and only two desert eagles, was sure enough a suicide mission and would be the death of me. It was all good because he will see me one day, and I'm going to make him pay.

TASI

I had been with Tony for a week and it was time for me to go home. I enjoyed his company and all, but the money was calling me. I had just gotten a call from *Queens in Style Magazine* to do a shoot for their cover. I was excited. I had to pack for a trip to New York, which was leaving in the next hour, so I had to pick up the pace. My phone was going off so I hurried to get it off the table. I didn't look at the number I just spoke.

"Hello?" I said.

The caller screamed, "Bitch, you think you doing something but you ain't. Stay the fuck away from Tony bitch, or you're going to see me," then hung up. I was smiling but still trying to figure whom the bitch was and how she got my number. Bitches kill me always claiming something that ain't theirs. I was hood but I try to keep it classy. I have an image to protect now, being a plus-size model whose name was known worldwide; I didn't want to tarnish that. I worked too hard to get to the top and I wasn't going to let a hood rat be my downfall. Messing with a hood nigga had its cons, but fucking with a chick had to be worst at times. Women are sometimes hormonal which causes a lot friction, and sometimes made me wonder why I loved pussy so much.

Star had been hitting me up all week, acting crazy because she knew I was with Tony, but I wasn't in a relationship with her so I really didn't care. Star was becoming clingy and I didn't like that shit at all. Ever since I became a model, she got worse. I guess she wanted a piece of the cash flow but she wasn't getting any. The only ones that were going to benefit from this were my mother, Lyana and I, and my babies at the daycare. Tony was about his money so I didn't have to worry about carrying him financially.

As I was headed to my car getting ready to go to Charlotte-Douglas International Airport, I called Lyana. I'm glad my little hookup had worked between her and Mex. My girl was happy again and she needed that, because her love life was in the dumps after Desmond fucked up. She picked up on the second ring.

"What's up ladybug, how are you doing?" I asked her.

"It's going good, I'm headed to my parents' house right now. You know I haven't been home in a week, let alone seen my parents. My dad is having a fit just as well as my mom."

"Girl, I know, Mrs. Tanya been blowing me up about you, but you know I would not tell on ya ass. But, you better get your ass over there ASAP. Ms. Tanya talking about filing a missing person's report on you," I told her. I was laughing hard because mamma Tonya didn't play about her girls and she really would put out a missing person's report.

"Tasi, I know she didn't say that shit did she?" Lyana asked. "If she did, shit just got real. You headed to the airport now?"

"Yeah, I am headed there now to catch my flight," I replied.

"Okay, call me when you land, love ya girl."

"Me without you and you without me, a never-ending story is all we'll be." We said our chant we had since we were little, and hung up the phone. I blasted my music as I headed to the airport, excited about my new adventure.

LYANA

My one night ended up turning into two weeks staying with Mex, and the sex was unbelievable. I still went to class every day and all, but I stayed with him at his crib. I mean to stay a week with me finally having the man I always wanted, was a dream come true. Now that we are an official couple, we didn't want to leave each other's sight. My parents were blowing me up on my cell, and not receiving an answer was driving them crazy. I have always jumped to my parents' every call and my not answering was a big no-no. After hearing Tasi tell me my mother was going to file a missing person's report, I knew I had to hurry to my parents' house. I drove to the East side to my parents' little mansion, and used my key to enter the home. I was in the kitchen getting something to drink out of the refrigerator, when my dad walked in with a mean mug on his face.

"Where the hell have you been and why in the hell haven't you answered your phone when your mother and I were calling you?" he asked. My dad had an attitude like one I have never seen in my entire life. My mom came into the kitchen, dropped all her groceries, ran up to me and hugged me as if I was in danger.

"I was so worried about you. You didn't answer your phone or anything," she said. She pulled me back so she could look over me as if she was looking for scratches and bruises. She told me never to do that again. "Please, at least text us and let us know you're okay."

"I will mom, but I am grown and I have my life."

"I don't give a fuck, you're still my little girl and you will call and text as such!" my dad yelled. He looked at me and said "Lyana, meet me in the cave, NOW!" My dad has never talked to me like that so I know shit just got real. I went to my dad's man cave and sat down in his favorite chair. He looked at me as if he were very disappointed.

"The word around town, Lyana, is that you have a little boyfriend. Is that true, Lyana, because if so, why do I have to hear about this in the streets?" I looked at my dad and saw the hurt he harbored, in his eyes.

"Dad, it wasn't like that, I was going to tell you and mom what was going on."

"So now you want to explain? Tell me how the fuck you're going to explain your name in the streets Lyana, and not only that, you defying me and your mom by hanging out with this thug ass nigga. What the fuck is going on with you, baby girl? You got more sense than this Lyana." I put my head down in shame because some of what my dad was saying was true, but I didn't think he would come down on me like that.

I had to think about my dad's sudden mood change. It was as if he had something against Mex or something.

"Lyana, I don't want you with that Mex boy and that's an order young lady. You will not see him again." My heart shattered into a million pieces. There was no way I was going to let my dad run my life. My dad ran East Charlotte but he didn't run me. I stood and told my dad I couldn't do that, I loved Mex.

He just looked at me and screamed, "You think you bad Yana, huh?" calling me by my nickname. "Well since you think you bad and he is better than me, GET THE HELL OUT OF MY HOUSE!" I ran to my car and cried. Never in my life did I think my dad would yell at me like that. This was like a movie, but I had a feeling this shit was going to end badly.

MEX

I just woke up and went to the bathroom to handle my hygiene. I got the phone and called Tony; we had to meet my dad at his crib, something very important. I put on my True Religion jeans, red Polo shirt, and my black and red Jordans. I decided I was going to drive my Range today, so I hopped in my 2015 Range sitting on 22's, and headed to my pop's place. I was hungry anyway and my mom always cooked a mean breakfast, so I was ready to eat. I pulled up and noticed my whole damn crew was in the spot. I had a feeling that some shit was about to go down. I didn't know what, but I was about to find out.

I walked in and my crew was in the kitchen eating breakfast. I dapped up my niggas and kissed my mom and little sister. My mom fixed my plate as I sat down at the table. A few moments later, my dad came in with my uncle Tony. My pops and uncle dapped up everyone and kissed my mother and sister.

"Mex, when you're done eating, meet me in the office," my father said. I finished my breakfast and headed to my pop's office to see what he was talking about. I entered his office and he was sitting at his desk, while my uncle sat in the recliner chilling.

"What's up pops, you wanted to see me?" I asked, sitting down in the chair in front of my pop's desk.

"Mex, I need to discuss some matters with you regarding your love life and the family business. First son, I heard you have a lady in your life that is taking some of your attention away. I know you're grown and all, but all you do is party and live it up of my gawd damn money and quite frankly son, I can't stand it anymore. Now, I don't know about the young lady you have in your life, but I do know about the family business.

Through the years, I knew you didn't want to be a part of this life, but I showed you the ins and outs of this game anyway. Now, all of your crew in there has been down with me for a good minute, and now it's time for you to jump on board son." I just sat there and listened to my dad because he was talking crazy, but then again, some of it was true. I didn't want any parts of the drug life and I wasn't planning on becoming a part of it neither. The only association I wanted with the drug empire is being the son of a drug lord, that's it, but now things were about to change and I don't think I'm ready for that just yet.

I just got with my lady and she knew I wanted no parts of this. I wonder if she would look at me differently. Lyana is a good girl, about to become a doctor, she wouldn't be interested in a dope boy, or would she? I heard good girls like bad boys, but that's not a chance I was willing to take.

"Dad, no disrespect or nothing, but what the hell are you saying to me right now? I can't join the family business right now, I don't know what to do. And this lifestyle ain't for me," I said.

"Look here Mex, I done taught you everything you need to know and now it's your time to shine son. I have waited for this shipment for a while now, just so I can take over Virginia and Georgia. This shipment wasn't supposed to be here for a couple of weeks, but plans got changed and you are going to help me son; I need you now more than ever."

"So, when is this supposed to take place Pops?"

"Tonight son, we need to catch the flight to Cali in three hours and right now you don't have a choice because you're coming with me." I thought to myself, *ain't this about a bitch, my whole life is about to change in three fucking hours.*

TASI

I landed at JFK airport, and was greeted by a limo driver, holding a sign with my name on it. I walked to him with my bags and he took them and said, "This way Ms. Weldon." I can get use this life. Well, I'm *going* to get use to this life because I deserve it. We pulled up to the beautiful hotel, much better than the ones in the 'lotte. The driver whose name I found out is Steve, said "Ms. Weldon" but I told him just to call me Tasi.

He said, "Tasi, you are staying in the penthouse suite." I was happy as hell that I was accommodated with such regards. When I got to the penthouse, I was holding my breath. The suite was huge. I had never seen such glamorous stuff in my life. The bedroom had a California king bed with a silky white and blue bed set, and the bathroom was his and her bathroom, showcasing a shower with eight showerheads, a Jacuzzi, and his and her toilets. I put my purse down and lay on the bed. It was so soft that I wanted to go to sleep on it right then, but I knew I couldn't because I had to be at the shoot in thirty minutes. I had to hurry up and handle my hygiene since Steve was waiting downstairs for me.

I made it to the shoot within a ten-minute block to be prepped up. Since I had enough time, I called Lyana and she picked up, on the first ring.

"Girl, what's up lady bug? I made it here to the big apple." I could hear sniffles like she'd been crying. "Lyana, what's up, you okay girl?" I asked which was dumb, because my bestie never cried unless it was serious.

"Tasi, girl, I'm catching the next flight coming to New York, I need you right now. My life is crazy and my dad has lost his everlasting mind. Please text me the info to the hotel, I will be there when you get there. I got to get the hell out of Charlotte before I put all of my years of training, to use." I knew Lyana was serious by the way she was talking; she never talked like that. We were both lethal with the shit we knew how to do, but Lyana was certified. I needed for her to get here. I know firsthand how Lyana can get once she gets in her hood stance. I would not wish that on my worst enemy.

Everyone thought Lyana and I were sweetest people around the way, but we had a dark side and we wanted to keep it there because we were treacherous and really, no one could fuck with us. I remember in middle school a girl named Felicia and her cousin, Shonda always picked on me because of my weight. They would tease me, trip me, throw things at me and even spit on me. Yes, big bad me, was bullied in middle school and I was new at the school, coming from Selma, North Carolina, a little town near Raleigh. I didn't want to make any more enemies, so I took the assault and never stood up for myself.

One day Felicia and Shonda cornered me in the bathroom. I'm claustrophobic, I don't like to be in tight places and when they did that, I pushed Felicia so hard she fell and bust her head on the sink. I couldn't believe I had just done that, I was shocked myself, but out of the corner of my eye, I saw Shonda coming for me. So, I closed my eyes waiting for the impact of her fist to my face. I never felt that punch because some girl was on Shonda beating the brakes off her. When she was finished, the girl looked at me and said, "Hi, I'm Lyana and I know your name is Tasi." I was lost because I thought everyone saw me as a nobody.

"Tasi, I've been waiting for you to put them in their place. I knew you had it in you, I can spot fighter a mile away." Lyana and I have been tight ever since. She told me to embrace my weight and love myself. That alone went so far because she made me believe in myself.

In high school, we were the shit. Our senior year was full of haters and we loved it, but you know it's one that will push you beyond your limits, and that was Felicia. She didn't get enough of the ass whooping in middle school, but Shonda didn't fuck with us at all. One day we were at the park and it was hot as hell outside. Yana and Desmond were on the bleachers kissing and hugging, as couples do. I was with Greg and his homeboy, sipping on some Goose. We were chilling, minding our own business. Felicia, Cha, Kim and

Ronda came by being messy as usual. Felicia yelled to the bleachers to Desmond.

"Thanks for the fuck last night; you really helped me relieve some stress boo." Lyana didn't even flinch she just sat there. She knew Felicia wanted a reaction but Lyana didn't make a scene.

She just looked at her and said, "No boo, thank you for giving my pussy a break. It's been sore every day this week." Everyone at the park was laughing at Felicia and she was so embarrassed, she ran to her car and left her girls standing there. Later that night, Yana and I were walking to the little mini mart on the South side of town. We saw Felicia walking by herself from the store.

"Look at that bitch, Tee," Yana said calling me by the nickname everyone called me.

"I see her. What's up Yana, what you trying to do?"

"Tee, I'm about to handle that bitch. Go get the car and meet me by the path." I did what I was told. When I got to the path, Felicia was knocked out cold. "Pop the trunk, Tasi and let's go to the woods." We rode to the woods in silence. We were in training to defend ourselves and in the training, we learned all kinds of shit, so I could only imagine what was to come.

Once we got to the woods, we parked where no one could see the car. I popped the trunk and Felicia was still knocked out. Lyana and I got Felicia out and started walking. We came up on this warehouse I never knew about, and I was shocked. Once inside, all kinds of guns, garden tools and chemicals were in there. We put Felicia in a chair in the middle of the floor, and tied her up. Yana got some water and dashed on her to wake her up. When Felicia came to, she saw Yana and I and started to scream, but we knew no one could hear her out here.

Yana got close to her and said, "So you think fucking people men is cute, huh? I'm about to teach you some morals in how not to fuck another woman's man." Yana pulled out a machete and said, "Tee, take the bitch's shoes off. Since she's fucking people's men, she should be able to afford a pedicure." I did what she asked. I had never seen Yana like this. It was as if she were the grim reaper himself. Yana started laughing.

"Tee, this bitch can't afford a pedicure and talking about she's a bad bitch." She pulled back that machete and cut both her feet off with one slice. Felicia screamed out in so much pain I felt sorry for her, but in a way, I loved seeing the pain in her eyes. Yana threw the machete and grabbed the wire cutters off the table. "And this bitch got her fingers painted, Tee. But, you touched my man with these hands bitch." One by one, she was cutting Felicia's fingers off, singing the nursery school rhyme "This Little Piggy."

"This little piggy went to the market, this little piggy stayed home, this little one wanted Roast Beef, and this little piggy wanted none, and this little piggy cried wee, wee, wee, all the way home."

Felicia was crying so hard. She was screaming how sorry she was and if we let her go, she wouldn't say anything. Yana said, "I know you won't say nothing because I'm going to make sure of that." She grabbed a jar with some clear fluid in it. She started to pour it over her legs and the skin started to fall off; that was some nasty shit. Then she looked at Felicia and said, "Bitch, learn to keep your mouth closed," and poured it down her throat. Her eyes started to pop out her head and her body split in two. Like I said, I know firsthand what she is capable of so I know she needed to get out of Charlotte ASAP.

MEX

As I was on a plane to California, my mind was in a million places, especially about the shit that's about to go down. I have been calling Lyana since this morning, but she kept sending me straight to voicemail and I wasn't feeling that shit. We are supposed to be in the climax of our relationship since it was new. However, it felt like it was fucked up because of the situation that was going on. I called and was sent to voicemail again. Tone came and sat beside me and said, "Yo Mex, what's going on with you man? I know you ain't down about this trip bro, you know I got your back."

"Nah Tone, it ain't that, Lyana ain't picking up the phone. I think something is wrong man."

"I feel ya man, and it might be, because Tasi just hit me up saying Lyana was catching a flight out there tonight," Tone replied, shocking me.

"Really? Man, somethings gotta be up 'cause she sending me straight to voicemail. I know she had to go to her parents' house because they were blowing her up. I guess something must have happened there since she's catching a flight to be with her bestie. Damn, my mind fucked up bra, I don't think I can do this. I'm not ready. In addition, my relationship seems to be failing before it gets started."

"Mex bra, I feel ya man, we going to get through this. But, I need you to stay focused man and let's get this shit done. Then we can catch a flight to the Big Apple to see what's going on." Tone was right; I needed to be a man about this situation.

We finally landed at Los-Angeles International Airport. I didn't understand why my dad didn't take his jet, but whatever we are here now. We had three Lincoln Navigators waiting in the parking deck. My dad, Killer, Tone and I rode together. I was a nervous wreck because I never thought I would be in this situation. We drove about two hours before we reached the docks. At the docks, there were men standing with machine guns around a black yacht. As we boarded the yacht, we were patted down, stripped of our guns and led to the back. There were three Asian guys, two dressed in black Armani suits and the other man was dressed in a white Armani suit. The man in the white suit began to speak to my dad.

"I see you made it my dear friend, let's get to business, shall we?" He got up and said, "This way gentlemen," and led us downstairs where the 200 bricks of uncut cocaine and 400 pounds of weed were, which was a small amount, but my dad had a plan for the weed.

My dad took two duffel bags from Killer and put them on the table. One of the Asian men that were dressed in black unzipped the bag, and nodded his head to his boss. Tone and I got the okay from Pops to start packing the product. I was happy as hell just to know my pops, uncle and my crew was in one piece. Once we got back in the truck, I had a text from Yana saying she was okay and will call later. I didn't want to hear that, I needed my girl, I wanted to hear her voice.

Before we pulled off, the Asian man with the white Armani suit, whom I just found out was named Voe, came to the truck and knocked on the window.

"Sambo, nice doing work with you, but your enemy is very aware of what has taken place. Keep your ears to the streets and eyes on the prize my friend," he said then he walked away. I was wondering what the old man meant but in the drug game, enemies were like a package deal. I just hoped my dad would be careful. We got back to the airport and I don't know how my dad got through with all the drugs he had on him, but whatever he did it worked.

My pops came up to me and said, "Son, we needed to start handling business. Mex, you are going to run here while your uncle and I will run Georgia and Virginia. We will work out the details later. We have to celebrate tonight son, you made me a proud father tonight; having your only son on the side of you doing something major, is nothing but love. I love you Mexquan, time to celebrate you joining the family empire and becoming a man."

"Let's just do this tomorrow, I'm tired, we all are. Let's set up a party for tomorrow, better yet, this weekend. It will give us time to get everyone together," I said.

"Okay son, that's a good idea. I love ya. Your uncle and I are going to drive around a little since we got a three-hour delay." I had to tell my pops something. I know he was happy for me joining the team and all, but all I wanted was to do was get to my girl. Tone and I got our tickets and were on our way to the Big Apple.

KILLER

The words that Voe said to Sambo kept playing in my mind. I knew the enemy had to be Cappo; he was once one of our brothers. I don't know what the beef was between him and Sambo, but I knew it had to be deep for him to up and leave the family like that. I was close to Cappo but my loyalty was with Sambo. When Cappo became the enemy to Sambo, he also became mine, even though I really didn't know what the deal was. Cappo was our competition, only in the 'lotte though, because his drug empire didn't extend past locally. At first, Cappo was going to start a war over the East side, but Sambo said "let him have it, he's local while we expanding worldwide." However, the word in the streets was Cappo was expanding out West and was trying to get some of the Northeast.

"Sambo, what you think about what Voe put in your ear earlier?" I asked.

"I have a feeling that nigga, Cappo is being sneaky, and I'm not feeling that shit at all," Sambo replied. I understood what Sambo was telling me because I was having the same feeling. I can't put my hand on it but I know some shit is about to go down.

TASI

My photo shoot went great. I was the cover of *Queens in Style Magazine*, as the new plus-size model. It was late and I was ready to hit the sheets. Earlier, I had sent Tone a text to let him know what was going on, and I told him my bestie was coming to New York. I know I'm tired and all, but as I entered the limo I could have sworn I saw Star and Cha. The drive to hotel was dreary. I had already called to tell the front desk that Lyana was coming and to let her in. I got to the hotel and took the elevator to the penthouse. Lyana was up in the living room, watching TV and eating ice cream.

"What's up boo, what's going on with you Yana?"

"Tee, I went to my parents' house 'cause I know since being with Mex I've been a little distant, plus you know they were blowing up phone some kind of crazy. I got there, went to the kitchen to get something to drink and my dad comes in. Tee, the vibe I was getting from him was a dark soul. I never felt a vibe like that; it was scary as hell. My mom came in, hugged me and told me she was worried sick about me and for me always to call or text to let them know I was okay. Any who, my dad wanted me to come to his office. Once I got there, his mood changed completely. Tee, that wasn't my pops. I don't know who that person was but I didn't like him. He told me that I could not see Mex again and that was an order it was like he was so ashamed of me or something.

I told him I love Mex and I could not do that. Girl, he kicked me out his house. I mean he literally raised his voice at me," Yana said, the pain evident in her voice.

"Wait Lyana, you telling me that Papa that I know raised his voice, yelling and demanding you not to go out with Mex and told you to get out? Yana, it has to be more to this story and you need to find out like ASAP. Did you at least talk to Mex about this situation?"

"Tee, I haven't talked to him. My dad's words kept playing in my head and I just couldn't talk to him, but I shot him a text letting him know I was okay."

"Yana, that's not fair you taking your anger out on that man because of a fuck up your pops made. That ain't right. You're making him suffer for something he ain't do. I bet he's worried sick about you and you're making him suffer, for what Yana. Call that man; I know he cares about you. Don't fuck this up because you want to be stubborn. Let him know what's going on, at least give him that much respect," I told her.

"Tee, you're right man, I love you girl and I don't know what I would do without you."

We looked at each other and said, "Me without you and you without me, a never-ending story is all we'll be." I got up to call Tone and heard a knock at the door.

"Tee, someone is at the door, you expecting someone?" Yana yelled out.

"Nah, I wasn't expecting anyone. It may be housekeeping or something, answer the door."

MEX

Looking at my baby come to the door with a messy ponytail and a Pink outfit on, had a nigga's mind racing. I just grabbed her face and started kissing her without as much as a hello. I missed my baby something terrible and I wanted to show her just how much. I forgot where the hell I was at for a minute, until I heard Tasi's ass telling me excuse her, as she was trying to get to Tone's black ass.

"Well damn Mex, hello to your ass too," Tasi said to me.

"I apologize, Tee, I was happy to see my girl, you know what I mean."

"Whatever nigga, get in here and out my damn doorway with your rude ass." Tee had a mouth on her but that was my little sis.

"Mex, how the hell did you know where I was and what the hell are you doing here?" Yana questioned.

"Yana, I can feel something is going on with you. What's up man? You sending me simple ass texts and straight to voicemail, that shit is a dub. We need to talk baby girl, because we in this shit together. It ain't no more you and I, it's us."

"You are right, baby, we do need to talk about what's going on." Lyana grabbed my hand as we headed to the guest bedroom, and sat on the bed.

"Talk to me baby girl, let me in. Yana, you got a nigga doing shit I've never done before. I was worrying myself sick and shit, you got my crew looking at me differently. They're running around talking about cupid shot me in the ass and shit." Yana started laughing.

"Ain't nobody said that crazy ass shit, but Los' crazy ass," and she was right.

"But any who, I'm feeling the hell out of you and I'm here for you one-hundred percent. Don't shut me out, baby. I need you in my life, you complete me," I said. Lyana gave me a kiss and started talking.

"I went by my parents' and my dad asked me to come in his office. Once I got in there, my dad's mood was completely off the charts. He was yelling at me and shit, and told me it was an order that I couldn't be with you, but I stood up to him. I told him I couldn't do that because I love you. When I told him that, my dad kicked me out of his house." When Yana told me that shit, I just held her tightly; that shit crushed a nigga's heart. It had to be more to this story.

I pulled her back, looked at her and said, "Yana, it's got to be more to this story. I don't even know your pops, who is he?"

She looked at me and said, "My dad is Cappo." That threw me for a loop. I heard of that nigga, he was a third part of my dad's squad, but my dad told he wanted to be greedy and start his own shit.

"Yana, did you know your dad used to be part of my family empire?" She looked at me confused. I could tell she really didn't know so I left that alone. I had to tell her I just joined my family's empire. I just hope and pray we still be together after this. "Bae, I have something tell you and I know ain't going to like it," I grabbed Yana's hand, "I joined my family's business today. I really had no choice." I was about to keep going to plead my case, but she stopped me in mid-sentence and started kissing me.

I started rubbing on her nipples and unbuttoning her shirt. I took her nipple in my mouth and started sucking it as if I were a newborn. She unzipped my pants and I stripped, as she got on her knees before me and started sucking my dick. My baby was a pro now. I taught her how to suck my dick and she loved it. She made me feel like no other woman had in my life. I was about to cum. She had a nigga feeling so good I was standing on my tiptoes. I released all my semen in her mouth and she swallowed every last drop. That shit was a major turn on for me.

I lifted her up, opened her legs and began to suck on her swollen clit. My baby was pushing on my head so hard, I didn't know if I should try to breathe or tap the hell out. I heard my bae say she was about to cum, so I sped up my licking and sucking on her pearl. All of a sudden, I felt a splash of warm liquid on my face; the shit felt good. My baby had squirted all over my face. That was a first, but I licked it all up. I could tell she was shocked her herself.

I told my bae to get on all fours and she obeyed. I wanted her so badly. At first, I was going to make love to her, slow-rolling style. However, she said she wanted some thug loving, so I put it to her long and fast. I mean, my baby was a beast in the bed. She was taking the dick like she was a porn star. She kept telling me to go faster so I obeyed. An hour and a half later, she was drenched in sweat and I released my seeds in her. I had forgotten my damn condom again, but this time I really didn't care. She was my love and I was going to do everything she wanted me to do.

I went in the bathroom to handle my hygiene and she came behind me. Yana looked at me and said, "I take you as you are... all I ask is you take me as I am." She gave me a kiss and said, "I'm your Queen and you're my King and it's us together." I kissed her and we were back in the bed on our way to sleep, until we heard Tone moaning and shit. We fell out laughing and before you know it, we were out for the count.

TASI

I was surprised when I saw Tone at the door. I had told him where I was, but I didn't think he would fly up here to see me. I was far from the relationship type. I was the 'like to have my cake and eat it too' kind of girl. However, I was falling for Tone. He catered to my every need; plus, his sex game was on point. I had just got out of the shower, smelling like cocoa oil. I was tensed and stressed at the same time. I was applying lotion to my legs when Tone took the bottle from me and said, "Let me handle that." I gave him the bottle as he began to lotion my body down, before telling me to lay on my stomach in the bed.

I guess he knew what I needed because he began to massage from my shoulders down to my ass, thighs and feet, working his down back up. While massaging me, he asked, "Tee, why don't you give a nigga a chance? You know I'm feeling you, ma. I know got your own bread, so do I, but I just want to love you, take care of you and call you mine. I know you about to blow up and shit, I want to be by your side to protect you from harm's way. I love you ma, give me a chance."

After he said that, he began to eat my pussy from the back. It was feeling so good I had to re-position myself on the bed. I wanted to feel all the warmness of his tongue. I reached over, grabbed my banana pudding clit gel, and poured it on my clit while he was eating my pussy. It must have been good to him, because he went in on my pussy as if he were mad at it or something. Tone was doing something mysterious to my pussy. We'd been messing around for a while, but never like this; he was giving me his all.

My body started shaking as if I were having a seizure. This was a first for me. I usually do this to men and women. Right then and there, I decided Tone was going to be my man. As soon as I squirted all over his face, I got up and ran to the kitchen, telling him to stay there.

"What the fuck, Tee?" he said. I went in the refrigerator grabbed the whipped cream, strawberries and ice. I was going to do some things to him tonight. This was going to be a night to remember. I was on birth control, a very effective one, so I really wasn't worried about him having a condom. When I got back, he was naked as the day he was born, with his dreads up in a bun on top of his head. I put my items on the floor where he could not see them, and crawled on top of him with the whipped cream in my hand, spreading it on, then kissing and licking every part of his body. I asked him to slide down to the edge of the bed. He did what he was asked to do. I picked up a strawberry, put whipped cream on it, and told him to take a bite and lay back down. I took the strawberry and put it in mouth with two ice cubes, chewed it a little bit to get the flavor, and started to suck his dick. Tone was moaning like a bitch but that shit turned me on. He started fucking my mouth slowly, but with perfection. He was screaming, "Bae, what are you doing to me? Tee, man, what in the world! Oh my gawd Tee, I'm about to bust." Just then, he busts in my mouth hard as hell and I swallowed every drop.

He lifted me up and told me to bend over and touch my toes. I'm fat, but very flexible. He dicked me down so good I had to tap out, but that didn't mean shit to him. "Nah Tee, you going to hang with big daddy tonight, now get on the bed, lay down on your back and hold then damn legs back, Tee. If you let go, I'm going to hit you harder, don't play with me." Tone's ass was putting it down I can't lie.

I slipped up and let go of my leg. That nigga had me speaking Spanish or some shit. He was hitting me so hard I had forgot all about English and had tears of passion running down my face. I screamed, "I'm cumming bae!"

He said, "Cum for daddy baby, I'm cumming right behind you." We bust together at the same time, laid down and were out.

STAR

I had followed Tasi to New York to confess my love for her. I brought my cousin, Cha along with me, just for support. I was so in love with Tasi it was crazy. When she wasn't answering my calls, I felt betrayed. I knew she was with that nigga, Tone and that shit alone was not sitting well with me. I had gotten with Tasi at a very low point in life, and she helped me out a lot. I was selling my body for drugs and a place to stay. I ended up getting hooked on drugs because the nigga I was with named Reese got a bitch hooked on that shit and left me high and dry. I had self-esteem issues and was very depressed.

I met her one day as she was coming out of the grocery store. I asked if she had any change. She looked at me at me and said, "Ma, why you out here looking like this, you too pretty ma." I held my head down in shame as she handed me some money and said, "Get yourself together, I see potential in you boo. The next time I see you ma, I better see you better than this because you're too gorgeous, baby," then she left. The words she spoke to me haunted my ass, and I got up the courage to sign myself into a drug treatment program.

Tasi had given me 1,000 dollars. I was grateful for her and her words. I held on, to her money, got myself cleaned up, and made up in my mind not to go back to my old ways. I stayed in rehab for six months. Once I got out, I got a studio apartment with the money I received from Tasi. I also picked up a gig at the strip club making hella cash. I was living well thanks to her.

One at night at the strip club, I was heading on stage after the DJ called my stage name, Delicious. I was on stage doing my thing and that's when I spotted Tasi and her crew. I put on my best performance and the crowd went crazy. I did my final act, as I climbed the pole, turned upside down with a beer bottle in my pussy, and slid down the pole with beer coming out my mouth. The crowd was going wild and money was flying everywhere. I picked up my earnings and headed to the back to get dressed, so I could meet up with Tasi. I had 6,000 dollars that night and I was going to hand Tasi her 1,000 dollars back.

I went to the bar where I spotted her.

"Hey, how are you?" I asked. She embraced me a hug and a smile.

"I told you the next time I see you, you better look good, and I must admit I like what I see Ms. Delicious," she replied.

"Actually, my name is Star, and yours is?"

"My name is Tasi."

"Nice to finally to meet you and here, this is for you," I told her as I handed her 1,000 dollars.

Tasi looked at the money said, "Nah, you keep that." I wanted her badly but didn't know how to approach her, because she didn't come off as a lesbian or a stud. Nevertheless, the way she was looking at let me know she liked what she saw.

"Tasi, since you don't want the money, let me thank you another way," I said. That leads us to today.

That night, Tasi had me climbing the walls, even though I initiated the shit. We had been rocking for a year now. Although she was bisexual and had options, I was greedy and didn't want to share. I had been an option for a year and that shit was getting old. Now that Tasi was a plus-size model with fame, I knew she would be making hella cash and I wanted in. I wanted to be on her arm and for the world to know she was mine. I saw those niggas, Tone and Mex going in the hotel where she was staying. I was livid. I had to off this Tone from messing with my woman. Tasi was my come up and no one was going to get in my way, not even Tone.

CHA

Coming to New York with Star, I really wasn't feeling that shit because I wanted some dick, but if the shoe was on the other foot, I knew she would have done the same for me. I was more than ready to head home really. I hated Lyana and Tasi, but I didn't really want no beef with them because my fight game was garbage. I had a lot of mouth but couldn't fight a lick, that's why I hung with bad girls because I knew if I had a fight, they would be behind me one-hundred percent.

When I saw Mex walk in the hotel, I knew he was going to see Lyana. I hadn't talked to Mex since he cut me off from sucking his dick, which was the day he took me shopping some months ago. I tried to get at him through different people, but that was a dead issue. I knew I shouldn't have put that post up about us, but a bitch was feeling herself. I had to get back on his good side or force him to see my point of view. Even though I knew I could never be his girl, I at least wanted some attention from him. Just to suck his dick had a bitch like me in love, and he hadn't really ever touched the pussy like that. I know the streets talked, but if they only knew, I was only his personal dick sucker and nothing else. I knew everyone was looking at me like I was crazy, but I really didn't give a fuck; I loved him. I was going to have the attention I deserved. I was even willing to suck his dick after he would fuck Lyana every night. Yes, I was a nasty bitch that wanted *that* man *that* much; I was willing to do anything to make him happy.

LYANA

When I woke up the next morning, Mex was beside me snoring like a baby cub. He was looking so cute I didn't want to wake him up. I headed to the bathroom and thanked God they had new toothbrushes. I handled my hygiene, took a hot shower and went back to the room. As soon as I opened the door, Mex was standing there butt ass naked, looking sexy as hell. I said, "Excuse me bae," as I walked past him. He moved to the side to let me by. I went to the closet and I heard the shower running, so I knew he was handling his business. I found my black Gucci sundress with my matching black Gucci sandals, a red panty and bra set from Victoria's Secret, and laid it out on the bed. I started to lotion my body with my favorite Sweet Pea lotion from Bath & Body Works, when Mex came out the shower and sat on the bed next to me.

"Hey L, I want you to know whatever the beef that our pops' have has nothing to do with us, and we are going to be together regardless." I admire a man with muscle; just talking to him, made me feel better. I knew that I had to face my dad sooner or later, but I will cross that bridge when the time comes. Mex asked me to go get his bag for him.

Tasi said, "Y'all hurry up so we can eat breakfast. I want us all to go to my press meeting today. I also want y'all to go with me on *The Real Talk Show*."

"Okay Tasi, I'm dressed, Mex will be ready in a few." I took Mex his bag and went back in the kitchen where Tee and Tone were.

"Hey, what's up with all the smiling this morning, Tee? You glowing boo, but not the pregnant glow, the happy glow, what's going on?" I asked.

"Well, if you must know nosy, Tone and I are an official couple," Tasi replied. I was lost for words.

"My girl finally on her grown woman shit, I see."

"First off all Yana, I been grown, but Tone sat my ass down a little bit," she said. I was happy for my girl. I knew Tone was a good guy. Even though he was a dope boy, he wasn't with every chick around the way. He kept to himself and focused on money. Mex came out the back with some True Religion cargo pants on and a black Gucci shirt with black Forces. He tried to match my fly. Tee's phone rang. After listening for a brief moment, she said, "Okay," then hung up.

"Okay y'all, that was Steve, he's downstairs waiting for us. Y'all ready?" We packed up and headed out to start our day.

New York was so beautiful. Taking in the sights on our way to the press conference, I had fallen in love with New York. We got out of the limo and there were so many camera people and paparazzi was everywhere. My girl was doing it big and I was so happy for her accomplishment. Tee and Tone were taking pics as newscasters asked what the relation between her and Tone was. She introduced him as her man. My girl was happy and beautiful at the same time.

The press conference was about two hours but we enjoyed every minute of it. When Tasi got off the stage, we all were headed to the limo to go to *The Real Talk Show*. I could have sworn I saw Star and Cha in the crowd, but there were so many people, I brushed it off a little bit. I love *The Real Talk Show* because I loved me some Tamar Braxton.

After the show, I got a chance to meet all the cast members. They were just as real as your average person was, and down to earth. I had fun and enjoyed myself. We were headed out to eat. We all were hungry so we decided to walk around a little bit to find somewhere to eat within close proximity. We saw this upscale Mexican restaurant. The food was great and we were beyond tired. We called Steve to pick us up and he arrived five minutes tops. We got in and headed to the hotel. Once we were in the room, we all plopped down on the couch, tired as hell, but it was well worth it, seeing the smile on Tee's face. I wanted to talk to Tee alone and the boys wanted to catch up on some football, so Tasi and I headed to her bedroom. We both sat on the bed.

"Tee, I can't believe this, you are a super model girl, but aye, you deserve it all baby girl. Hey, I don't want to scare you or nothing, but I swear I saw Star and Cha earlier today," I informed her.

"Yana you not tripping, 'cause I saw the same thing the other day. I wonder what that's about. Girl, I hope they ain't trying to start some shit because they don't want these problems."

CAPPO

I knew that nigga Sambo had just copped a shipment. I knew all too well what that kind of product could do. Those niggas, Sambo and Killer thought I was just a local nigga, but I was not. I was the man behind the scenes to a lot of big dope dealers, in addition to being the Connect for the West Coast. My wife's uncle, Papi is the Cuban drug lord and my supplier. I could have been killed Sambo for the shit he did to Tanya, but I decided not to and chose to hit him where it hurts the most, his pockets. If you hit a man's pockets, he can't flow in the streets and can't provide for his family. A man without muscle is like a poor man on the streets. I've been waiting for this moment for a while. I was going to have that nigga begging and pleading, that's if I didn't kill him first.

The fact that Lyana hadn't called, had me feeling some type of way. As a father, you're supposed to protect your child. Lyana was my only girl, my first-born, and I would do anything for her. I have a son, Cappo Jr. He was a product of what happened between Tanya and Sambo. He is eighteen years old and a wild child in the streets. For some reason, him and Lyana didn't get along, never have, until it was some beef that needed to be handled with some females, which was very rare.

I knew I had no reason to be mad at Lyana, but I couldn't stomach the fact another Sambo was entering my family yet again. I had to swallow my pride. My wife had to really sit down and talk to me. I had to bite the bullet. I never told my kids what went on with Sambo and his family empire, and I wanted it to stay like that. I had a bad feeling I might be regretting that situation. I called Lyana to tell her I apologize, but I knew she wouldn't pick up the phone, so I shot her a text telling her what I wanted to say. Shit was about to get real, so I had to get my priorities together, which meant my family.

LYANA

My vacation in New York lasted a week long, but we've been back in North Carolina for two weeks now and I still hadn't spoken to my dad. I was at staying at Mex's since we've been back; it almost felt like I moved in. My graduation was in the morning and we set a party for tomorrow night. My mom was coming but I don't know if my dad was coming to be a part of my day. I was heading out because I had a doctor's appointment. I had been feeling sick since yesterday.

I hopped in Mex's 2015 Range Rover. As I was heading to the doctor, my phone went off indicating I had an incoming text. I grabbed my phone and it was a text from my dad, apologizing for his behavior. I really needed that because I was truly a daddy's girl. I don't talk about my brother much, because we don't get along too well. I wished sometimes that we had that sister- brother relationship. The only time we got along was when we were fighting other people. I arrived at the doctor's office, went to the front desk and told the receptionist I had a three o'clock appointment. She handed me some forms to fill out, and told me to have a seat and wait for my name to be called. As I finished the paperwork, I heard the bell chime and looked to see who was coming through the door; it was Mex. He was standing there smiling like a Cheshire cat.

"What are you doing here? I thought you was out handling business, bae?" I asked.

"Lyana, you are business, now let's wait 'til the doc calls you." I heard the nurse say, "Ms. Duhtrum, the doctor is ready for you."

After going to the exam room, shortly after the doctor came in and asked what was going on with me. I told him that I'd been sick and throwing up. He gave me a cup for a urine sample and said to give it to the nurse. He also told me to let the nurse look over me and he would be right back. The nurse checked my blood pressure and said, "Your blood pressure is high, Ms. Duhtrum." The look in

Mex's eyes let me know he was worried.

The doctor came back in and said, "Ms. Duhtrum, you are three weeks pregnant."

"Doc, that can't be right because I took the morning after pill," I said.

"You may have taken it a little too late, or maybe God wanted this to happen, Ms. Duhtrum." I was worried and Mex was happy as hell. The doctor told me to get plenty of rest, and try not to stress, since my blood pressure was high and it wasn't good for the baby, then handed me a slip for prenatal vitamins.

Thank God, I was graduating tomorrow and had a job waiting on me because otherwise, I would be stressing hard right now. I'm thankful for Mex, too, just being there, but I was worried about the family that was outside of our element. This could go good or end up very badly.

MEX

I was so happy my baby was having a baby. I was going to be a daddy. When the doctor told Yana those words, I wanted to dance. Life was moving fast for us, but maybe it was God's way of showing us something. I helped my baby get in the car and I got in mine, waiting for her to pull off. We were going to the pharmacy to get her pills. I was smiling hard, until my phone began ringing and I saw it was Cha. She had been hitting me up like ten times out of a day. That girl would not leave me alone. I was going to put her ass in a box floating somewhere. All she wanted was to suck my dick, but I wasn't feeling shorty no more. She was too messy for me, and I wasn't losing my wifey and unborn child for a thot.

I just let it ring, hoping the bitch got the picture by now, but she was a bug-a-boo. I was going to get me a new number. I pulled up at the pharmacy right after Yana. We got out, headed in the store, and got in the line to get her medicine. The lady said it would take ten minutes for it to be ready, so we walked around the store just to kill time. I saw a massage chair and some massage shoes. I picked them up. I wanted my baby to be relaxed and really didn't want her on her feet. Her big day was in the morning, so I really wanted her to be on point, meaning she needed to rest up. The lady said the medicine was ready, so we grabbed it and headed out to our cars.

I helped my baby into her car and she told me she was headed to my crib. I kissed her and told her I would be there later. I called Tasi to see if she was around, because I wanted someone there with her. Tasi picked up on the second ring. "Hey sis, are you around 'cause I need you to stay with Yana at the crib, if you don't mind; she's sick." Tasi said she was on the way. I told Yana, Tasi was on her way before I left. Once I got in the car, I received a call from Los.

"Get to the spot on Fuller and Westgate now, we've been hit hard," he said. Damn, I just couldn't have a good day, but who would be stupid enough to rob my stash house.

LOS

Ever since Sambo left North Carolina to Mex, things started to get real shady. These niggas in the streets were trying to test us hard. We had just got hit for fifty bricks… like, who the fuck would do some shit like that? I've been with Sambo for eight years and no shit had ever popped off, now all of a sudden, niggas getting greedy. I called Mex, Tone, Bug and Marcus because we needed to figure out who had the balls to rob us. I had a bad vibe something wasn't right about the crew, like we had a rat amongst us. Like B.I.G. would say "more money more problems".

I hope my vibe was wrong because I loved these niggas with everything in me. They are my kids' Godfathers. I had four kids, two boys and two girls. Carlos Jr., Jeremy, Connie and Marie were their names. I had been married to my high school sweetheart, Christy for nine years and she loves my brothers as if they were hers.

Mex, Tone and Bug pulled at the same time, but I didn't see Marcus. I thought he would be here by now, but he wasn't. I dapped up my boys and we headed in the house. "Los, tell me this shit is a joke man, what the hell is going on?" Mex was yelling.

"I don't know man, what the hell is going on. One of the little niggas that be at this spot said niggas rolled up three cars deep with ski masks on and machine guns.

"Where that nigga at Los?" Mex was heated and I could tell, because he was normally cool, but I knew he had to step up because he was now in the family business. I told him the nigga was in the back and I went and got him. Mex was looking the young boy named little Q, up and down, then he began to speak to him.

"Hey little nigga, tell me what you saw and don't miss a fucking thing. I want to know everything." Little Q was scared as hell. He was crying while telling Mex what he saw.

"I was standing on the stoop. The nigga Alan and I were posted up as we had been doing for two years now. Alan went to use the bathroom and I was out by myself. I was about to sit down, when I heard tires screeching. I looked up to see three trucks come to a stop and niggas with AK's jumping out, telling me to put my hands up. Alan came out the door and they let off a shot in his arm, and he fell down. One dude hit me in back of the head with the butt of the gun and I was out. When I woke up, the first thing I did was hit up Los and Alan's ass was gone," Little Q told Mex.

"Aight little nigga, the fact that you stayed here through that nasty ass gash in the back of your head, tells me you're loyal to me. As far as your dude, when I see him he's dead because I don't deal with disloyal motherfuckers. Bug, take the young nigga to go get some stitches."

Los, Tone and I were going to look for this nigga, Alan. The fact that Marcus was there and he wasn't answering his phone, had me thinking this nigga was a snake. "Aye, we need to switch spots in the morning; we're moving everything and switching every other day. We need security in all the spots. We need more men and loyal men on our team, people we can trust." I was going to catch up with these niggas. The fact alone that we had snitches was fucking with me hard.

LYANA

The next morning I was feeling a little bit better. The morning sickness had quieted down a little bit. I was hoping that it stayed that way all day. Today is my graduation and I was ready to cross the stage and become Doctor Duhtrum. Mex had laid my clothes out, and had rose petals and candles in the bathroom. He helped me out the bed and into the bathtub. He looked at me and said, "Today is your day, I'm going to cater to your every need, baby." I loved this man; he was my everything.

I picked up my phone and saw a group message from everyone saying that they would meet me at the auditorium at school. I washed up and Mex helped me a little bit. When I got out of the tub, Mex wrapped a towel around me and helped me to the bed. He dried me off and lotioned me down with my Sweet Pea lotion. He even dressed me, which I thought was so cute. We headed to Mex's Bugatti, got in, and he drove to the auditorium.

Everyone was there, my mom, dad, and brother, Tasi, Tone, Los and Bug. I didn't see Marcus, which was unusual, because they were all tight as hell. I was so happy everyone was there to support me. I took my position, along with my peers, waiting to be called to walk across the stage. As the dean called my name, I began to feel sick. I had to get to the bathroom. I walked across the stage and got my diploma. No sooner than I was getting off the stage, I ran to the bathroom, just in time to vomit in the toilet. My mom ran after me in the bathroom.

"Lyana, are you all right?" she asked me.

"Yes Mom, I will be alright. Maybe it's just that I'm overwhelmed with excitement." She gave me a look like she knew there was more to it than what I was saying, but I wouldn't tell her right now that I was pregnant. I wanted to wait until the right time.

We left out the bathroom and everyone was waiting to go celebrate. My dad was mean mugging the shit out of Mex, and I could not understand why. We all headed to Mex's house where we were celebrating my day. Everything was going smoothly, as everyone was getting to know each other. My dad was acting strange like he was so ready to go. My brother, Junior, came up to me and asked if we could talk for a minute. We went inside the living room and sat on the couch, as Junior began to talk.

"Yana, I love you sis, and over the years we haven't had the best relationship, to the point no one even knows I'm your brother. I know I be wilding out in these streets and shit, but I'm still your brother. I was so happy to see you walk across the stage. I'm not good at this talking thing, but I want us to have a better relationship." I was shocked but so happy. I loved my brother and at times, I needed him more than he would ever know. I told him I loved him, too, and we would have a better relationship from this day forward.

Mex yelled that the food was done and we all sat down to eat. My dad had a worried look on his face. I said grace and began to eat, as my dad said, "Excuse us Yana, your mother, brother and I have to go." It was obvious that he was in a rush.

"Okay Dad," I said as they got up to leave. I noticed something I hadn't before. I looked and my brother and back at Mex. It was like looking at his twin, they looked so much alike. It was borderline scary. "What the hell is going on?" is all I could get out, before my dad, mom and brother were out the door.

CAPPO

I had to hurry up and leave my baby girl's celebration because I knew shit would hit the fan soon. I knew of Mex, but seeing him, him and Junior could go for twins. Nobody really paid it any attention because everyone was enjoying themselves, but I peeped game when we got inside the auditorium. I was so tense I just wanted to skip the graduation all together, but I knew I couldn't do that. Tanya would have killed me and Yana would have never forgiven me. Junior was in the back seat asking all types of questions that I could not answer right now, but I knew sooner or later, I would have to. I got to the house in fifteen minutes, when it was usually a thirty-minute drive. I got out and Junior was yelling at me.

"Pops, what the hell was that? I look like I can be that nigga's brother, what the fuck is going on?" I couldn't even say anything, I didn't have a voice at that moment.

Tanya looked at me and said, "Cappo, it's time for them to know, if you don't tell them, I will."

"Okay baby, you're right, I will tell them. Call Lyana and Mex, tell them to meet over here in the morning." Junior didn't agree to what I was saying. He wanted answers now and before I could say anything, he sped off in his car. I knew he was headed back to Mex's house to try to get some answers that I knew he wouldn't get.

MEX

I swear I can't catch a break even if I tried. My girl is pregnant and stressing, one of my niggas is a snake, and to top things off, my girl's brother looks like he could also be *my* brother. I just wanted to enjoy my baby's graduation, but I guess that was asking too much. Lyana was stressing, I could see it in her face, and I kept thinking about what the doctor said, so I told her to go over Tasi's house until I figured what was going on. She had been gone for about an hour now and my niggas were still at the house trying to figure out the situation as well.

"Mex, man, that nigga got to be your bro. That nigga got to be something 'cause y'all niggas look just alike!" Tone was screaming. He was mad as hell, because all we could think about was someone had been lying to us about some shit.

Bug's phone started ringing and he picked it up. All I heard was, "keep them there, we will be there in a minute." and he hung up.

"Yo y'all, I just got a call from the fiend around the block. He just spotted Marcus and Alan on Park Avenue." My trigger finger was itching. I was ready to off them niggas.

We hopped in the Suburban and was about to pull off, until I saw headlights. I saw someone get out the car and come walking towards the truck. I couldn't see who it was until the person got closer; it was Junior. I could tell he had something on his mind, but right now wasn't the time to talk, so I just told him to get in. The ride to Park Avenue was quiet. My niggas knew how I moved. I had to concentrate and I wanted to be on point.

I parked down the street and hit the lights so I couldn't be seen. I parked behind seven cars but still had a good view of them niggas. They were laughing and talking like they knew each other for years. They were in front of a house sitting on a porch, then I saw them niggas get in a black Nissan Maxima and pull off. I followed those niggas. I made sure I stayed five cars behind so I wouldn't spook them. I followed them for an hour and thirty minutes, leading us into Durham NC. I didn't know what they were doing but I wasn't going to let them out of my eyesight.

They pulled up to some strip club called Sex Tease and I watched them go in. Whether or not they knew it, they had just fucked up. We waited about thirty minutes. I turned around and talked to my crew plus Junior.

"Look, this what we going to do. I'm sending Junior in there because they don't know him and shit won't be suspicious. When you get in there, get a lap dance from a bad bitch and tell her you want to buy two Long Island ice teas. Once she brings them back to you, send her on her way, while you slip these two pills in their drink. I know the niggas will drink it because that's Marcus' favorite drink.

Look Junior, don't fuck this up man, and make sure you get a different bitch to send the drinks to them niggas. We will be parked around back where no cameras are. When you see them niggas feeling the effect, go over there and get them niggas to come out the back entrance."

***

We waited about thirty minutes and boom, here comes Junior and them fuck niggas, out the back door. They were so fucked up they didn't recognize us. I picked up Alan and Tone picked up Marcus, and we threw them in the trunk. I drove back to Charlotte to my safe house. My crew got them niggas out and we headed straight to the basement. I tied Marcus up to the chair as Tone did the same to Alan. The effect of the pills was starting to wear off. Marcus' eyes grew big as hell, when he recognized where the hell he was at and the people before him. He had been to this room a time or two, so he knew what went down in here. Alan just looked confused until he saw Los standing there. He just started yelling, "HELP, HELP, HELP!" He could yell all he wanted to, but the basement was soundproof. Marcus just shook his head because he already knew, so he just snapped at him.

"Just shut the hell up motherfucker, no one is going to hear you," he told Alan. I looked at Marcus and asked him why and he said, "I'm not your servant anymore, you fuck boy. You and Sambo can suck my dick 'cause I ain't telling you shit." I knew he was telling the truth so I just let out two shots to his dome.

Alan began to cry, saying it wasn't him. Marcus told him if he did it he was going to give him a half a mil' to set me up. I was like really and then I thought, *who would give Marcus that kind of money just to knock me off my grind?*

"Nah little nigga, there is more to this story. Who sent y'all little niggas?" He was silent until I put my gun to his head. "I'm going to ask you more time or I'm going to send you to your maker. Who sent y'all little niggas?"

He looked up at me and said, "Cappo." I shot that nigga in the head and my crew and I drew our guns out on Junior.

JR.

My head had really been spinning since I really took a good look at Mex, and noticed how much we looked alike. My mom gave me a worried look in the car, on the way to the house from my sister's celebration. I kept asking my pops questions, but they fell on deaf ears. When I heard my mom say that it was time for me and my sister to know, I knew it had to be more to the story at hand. I got in the car and headed to Mex's house. Once I got there, he and his crew were headed somewhere; however, I wanted to talk to him. Judging by the mean mugs on their faces, I knew it wasn't the right time. I wanted to say go ahead but Mex told me to hop in.

Now after all that, the nigga Alan that Mex just offed, just told these niggas my dad had set them up. I had five guns pointed in my face and I was scared as shit. Los said, "Damn Mex, how many more snakes do we need to off?"

"I don't know, but we about to find out."

I looked over at everyone and said, "I don't what the hell is going on, but I don't have nothing to do with this. The only reason why I even came to you, is to find out the situation about you and me looking so much alike."

Mex put the gun to my head and yelled, "I should kill your ass right now! If it wasn't for the love I have for your sister and that fact I want some answers, I would light your ass up right now." They put down their guns, but I could tell none of them trusted me. I was tired and wanted go home. Mex made a call to his clean-up crew, and they were on the way.

We got in the car, but the drive was lonely and quiet back to Mex's house. I got a text from Lyana asking if I was okay. I texted her back letting her know I was. Once we got to Mex's house, I didn't even want to talk anymore I just wanted to sleep.

LYANA

(Six months later)

My stomach was huge, but being pregnant gave me so much joy. I was loving being a Pediatric Physician. I loved kids and now I'm about to bring a baby into the world. Today was the day Mex and I found out the sex of the baby. I'm seven months today. I was supposed to have been found out the sex, but working and being on call had me on the go.

Since the night of my graduation, I haven't seen nor spoken to my parents. Mex did find out one part of the family's secret. Junior and Mex went and got a DNA test a couple months back, and they were brothers. That shit was fucked up because Junior was also my brother, but on the contrary, our relationship got so much better. Mex and Junior were inseparable once they found out. The whole crew had gotten tighter; you couldn't pull them apart if you tried.

Tasi was doing it big. My girl was in Hawaii right now doing a movie called *Phat Girlz 2*. I was so happy for her. Tasi was flying in tomorrow for two weeks, and I needed to spend time with my best friend. We talked every day, but it was nothing like having her here. Mex and I arrived at the doctor's office, and the whole crew was there for support. I heard Marcus got killed in a drive-by shooting, him and some young cat named Alan. Mex didn't seem moved by the death at all but I never pressed the issue.

The nurse called my name to come to the back saying the doctor was ready for me. I have been having Braxton Hicks like crazy lately, but I knew that came with being pregnant, so I didn't pay it any attention. The doctor came in asked me how I was feeling, and I told him I was fine. Nevertheless, I did inform him about the Braxton Hicks.

"Let's take a look Ms. Dahtrum," he said. He began to put a cold solution on my stomach and moved the wand around to find the baby. He said, "First of all, y'all are having a boy and a girl." I only needed one baby, but two was so much better. Mex had tears in his eyes. He was about to go in the lobby to tell the crew the sex of the babies, but the doctor said, "Hold one minute son, there is more."

"More? What you mean doc?" I asked. "There is more as in I'm having more than two babies doc?"

"No, you're not having any more babies but you will be having these babies sooner than you think." Mex had a concerned look on his face. "Well Ms. Dahtrum, the reason why you are having so many Braxton Hicks is because the twins are in distress and I need to get them out now." I looked at the doctor like he had two heads on his shoulder. I wasn't ready right now. I needed my best friend and my mom. The doctor told Mex to head over to the hospital because he had to perform an emergency C-Section.

I called Tasi first and she was in tears. She stated she was on her way and taking the director's jet. I called my mom and she picked up on the first ring. I told her I just needed her there, everything else was irrelevant right now, and I didn't want my daddy there. She informed me he wasn't in town but she was on her way. The crew was so happy they had tears in their eyes. Los was a father of four, so he knew the feeling all too well.

MEX

I was scared, I didn't know what to do. I thought when you find out the sex of the baby, you get the pictures and head home. I thought I had a couple of months to prepare myself for the daddy role. I needed my mom and sister with me so they could help me out. I haven't spoken to my mom or my father either, since the graduation, but I needed her badly right now. I was getting ready to call her, when I looked at my phone and she was calling me.

"Hello?" I answered the phone.

"What's wrong?" she asked.

"Mom, how did you know something was wrong?" She told me because she was my mother and she could sense these things. I told her that Yana had to get an emergency C-Section because of the twins. She just said she was on the way and hung up. I didn't want my pops there because I wasn't feeling him at all. I was still searching for answers about Junior being my brother. Since we have gotten to know each other, I loved that nigga to death, and the crew loved him just as much. It's crazy how your life can change in a little amount of time.

We got to the hospital and went to the Labor and Delivery floor. The nurse asked for the patient's name. I told her while Lyana got into the wheelchair, and they took her to the back to prep her for surgery. The nurse grabbed my hand and took me to the back as well, to get ready for my babies' arrival. They gave me a gown, mask, shoes and gloves. I looked like I was going to perform the surgery myself. I heard a lot of commotion outside the door and went to see what was going on. My mom and Lyana's mom, were fussing out the nurses. I walked out and they ran to me, thinking I was a doctor asking is everything okay. I fell out laughing but that pissed them off. They were going in on me. I had forgotten I had on the whole scrub outfit.

I pulled down my mask and they fell out laughing. I told both of them to come to the back. The nurses also handed them the same items they had given me. Lyana was in the back screaming my name. I got back there and I could tell she was scared as hell. She told the doctors she didn't want be put to sleep. My mom and I were on one side of the bed and Lyana's mom was on the other, until Tasi came in. Lyana was so happy to see Tasi and her mom there. I knew how she felt, because I needed my support system too. Tasi had brought her video camera to tape the whole thing.

I was trying to be a man and see my seeds come into this world, but once I saw that hole in my baby's stomach, with so much blood around it, I fainted like a bitch. I woke up in a hospital bed next to Lyana and heard the soft crying of babies. Everyone was laughing at my ass, but I didn't care, I just wanted to hold my babies. I got off the bed, went to the beds the hospital had them in, and picked both of them up. I asked her what she named them. She said, "Nothing yet, I was waiting for you to wake up, to name them." I named them Anastasia Love Salvador and Antonio Lance Salvador.

My babies were both 7lbs even. They had pretty browns eyes and a head full of curly hair. I gave Anastasia the name because of Tasi and Love because her birthmark was a heart on her stomach. Antonio was because of my best friend Tone. I was happy I was going to make Lyana my wife because she been there for a nigga, a true rider. The nurse came in to check Lyana and the babies. We knew they needed their rest, so we all headed out to the waiting room. My boy, Los came and gave me a hug and said, "Welcome to the daddy club, Mex." He had to go do some family time, so he left.

Tone and Tasi were in the corner looking all lovey dovey and shit. Junior was on the phone but he whispered he needed to go handle something. I saw Bug in a conversation with my sister, Keshena, and it looked heated, so I approached them but everything got quiet.

"What was that all about?" I asked. They both said, "Nothing." I knew something was up but I just walked away. My mom and Lyana's mom were in the hall talking. I could see both of them had been crying.

As I was walking up, I heard my mom say, "Why didn't you

tell me Tanya? We were best friends. Regardless, you could have told me." That threw me for a loop because I didn't even knew my mom knew Mrs. Tanya. I asked was everything alright and my mom said, "No son, nothing is alright, and I don't think nothing will be after this."

CAPPO

I was happy of the news I had just received, about my baby girl giving birth to my grandbabies. I was also sad because I wasn't there to witness it myself. Things were so fucked between my family and me. I haven't talked to neither my son or daughter in six months. They were both staying at Mex's house. I felt like shit because I should have been a man and talked to my children about the things at hand, but I had chosen a coward's way out and just let shit hit the fan. I've been in Cuba trying to handle business with some Jamaicans. They wanted the New York territory and they had to have a good plan and a lot money to get that. My connect wanted to make sure things went according to plan, so we had to meet in Cuba.

I love my job as being the Connect; it had the benefits of being a president. I got the best of everything and I enjoyed every minute of it. I had them niggas, Marcus and Alan to rob Sambo. If I knew that I was robbing Mex, I wouldn't have done it so quickly. I was going to rob all the stash spots to take Sambo off his game. The fact that them fuck niggas were dead, I knew them niggas talked and Mex knew I had set him up.

I really wanted to stay out of his way because shit could get ugly real fast if I didn't. The fact that my son now knows that him and Mex were brothers, he's been all in Mex's ass, when he was supposed to be on the side of me growing my empire. I don't care if he was my son or not, if he wanted to side with the enemy, I would kill his ass, too, with my eyes closed.

I went to a little bar/café called Detomy. This spot was right off the beach away from everything. It was peaceful, or so I thought. I was drinking a Corona when I spotted a familiar face. This nigga had his gun and I pulled out mine, just as he let off a shot, missing my head by a couple inches.

KILLER

I had this bad chick I had been kicking it with for a couple of months now, named Star. She had a nigga wanting to settle down. She was a rider for real. Baby girl waited on me hand and foot so I felt it was only right to take her out of the country and treat her to the best life could offer. We had been in Cuba for a week and I could see myself living here. The people were so nice and the food was the bomb. I didn't really care for the clothes because I was a street nigga and their clothes wasn't cutting it for me. I had just given my shorty my black card to go shopping, to get some baby clothes. My Godson just became the father of twins, a girl and a boy, Anastasia and Antonio. I was so happy for him. I know him and his pops weren't seeing eye to eye right now, but I still love him like a son. I had heard that Cappo Jr. and Mex were brothers and that was puzzling me hard. Sambo never said anything about having sex with Tanya, and I knew for a fact Stella couldn't have known. But what I did know is that the fuck nigga, Cappo had set Mex up, and that was a big no-no in my book.

I saw that nigga sitting down at the bar and I was thinking, *this must be my lucky day*. I pulled my gun out and tried to hit that nigga in the head, but he fell back on the stool like the Matrix and I missed. I ran behind the table for cover, as that nigga let off back-to-back shots. He had them damn Beretta's; he loved them guns. I saw the nigga run to the back door, so I followed behind him. Once I got outside, the nigga had vanished. I was going to get that nigga though. He was going to see me either here or back in the states.

TASI

I was so in love with my God babies, I didn't want to put them down. I stayed with Yana for two weeks, helping her out since she got out of the hospital. Tone and I couldn't keep our hands off each other, either. I didn't want to leave but money was calling my name. I had just finished the movie *Phat Girlz 2* and my name rang bells, now that I was big time.

Star had called me a couple of times telling me she loved me, and Tone could not love me like she can. I told her I enjoyed what we had, but I was in love with Tone. She had called, texted and sent letters begging me to leave Tone so she could be with me, but that was months ago. I guess she finally got the picture to leave me alone. My flight leaves in five hours to go to Las Vegas, for a press conference about the movie. The good thing is, Tone is going with me on this trip. We would be gone for three weeks. I loved the fact that my man would go out of his way to make me happy. I love that man something serious. I really couldn't ask for a better man, he was my knight in shining armor.

The crew came over and chilled, and Los brought his kids and wife. My mom, Mrs. Stella and Mama Tonya, came in and went straight to the kitchen to start cooking. I didn't know the occasion, so I just went with the flow. I looked in the kitchen and it made me smile; my mom was all smiles. The ladies looked like they've known each other for years. They were enjoying each other's company like they needed each other in their lives. I heard the babies crying, so I went to pick them up, but my mom and Mrs. Stella beat me to them. It was like they were Speedy Gonzales or some shit, because I swear, they were just in the kitchen cooking.

A couple of hours passed and we were having a family day. I really enjoyed myself. When we got finished eating, Tone and I headed to pack our clothes to leave. When we got to the door, Tone got on one knee and pulled out the most beautiful engagement ring I had ever seen. It was a ten-carat cushion shaped ring.

"I never knew my life would get to this point but I can't see myself without you. You complete me so much, our hearts have the same beating pattern. I love you Shantasia 'Tasi' Weldon, will you marry me?"

I said, "YES, YES, YES baby, I will marry you!" Now I see why everyone came over, they all knew, but I wouldn't have it any other way than to be surrounded by love on a special occasion as this.

LYANA

Having my best friend around helping me with the babies for the past two weeks, was nothing but love. I love that girl more than life itself at times. When Tone came to me and said he wanted to propose and wanted everyone there, I was all game. Tasi deserved to happy and she got it, so as long she was happy, I was good. I was getting use to the babies being home, getting up in the middle of the night. We all took turns, Tasi, Mex and I. Now that Tasi was heading out, it would just be me and Mex.

I can honestly say Mex is a better father than I thought he would be. He was around the clock help, even helping change diapers. I had to give him his props. My mom and Mrs. Stella came a few times out the week to help. My mom said they were once was very good friends but something happened. However, since they've been back in contact, they have once again become the best of friends.

Today, since everyone was over to the house, Mrs. Stella and my mom wanted to talk to Mex, Junior, Keshena and I. After everyone left, we went into the living room to talk. My mom and Mrs. Stella stood up in front of us and said, "it's time y'all know how Mex and Junior are brothers." My mom started talking first.

"Cappo was in the Salvador Empire. He, Killer and Sambo were all like brothers. I was making more money than Cappo, being a lawyer and that didn't sit well with him, being the man of the house. He hooked up with Sambo to make a way for his family, because he felt embarrassed taking money from me, when I had Lyana and was providing for the household. He didn't want people to look down on him, so he took a job working with Sambo.

When the crew was always out, it was Stella and I, thick as thieves. Whenever you saw me, you saw her, that's how tight we were.

One day, Cappo had to make a trip on the West side of town for Sambo, to handle some Mexicans. I knew Stella was out shopping because I had just gotten off the phone with her. As soon as I hung up, I heard the doorbell ring. I looked out the peephole and it was Sambo. I didn't think nothing of it because he was like family, I thought he was just coming to check on me since Cappo was gone. I opened the door, he came in and we started talking. I was in the process of calling Cappo, so I turned my back to go into the living room, when I felt a gun to the back of my head. I was so scared I didn't know what to do, but I put my phone in my pocket so Cappo could hear what was going on.

Sambo told me to get upstairs and take off all my clothes. With the gun still to my head, he raped me. I didn't want to do it because I loved Cappo and Stella was my best friend. He told me if I told Stella, he would kill Lyana. I knew he was serious about it too. He raped me for about two hours, and came in me so many times. When he left, I went straight to the shower and tried to scrub my skin off. Cappo came home with his guns in hand. He saw me in the shower and got me out. He told me he had heard everything and he wanted to kill Sambo, but I didn't want my husband in jail or killed, so I asked if he would let it go.

Months had passed and I was feeling bad. I was sick, throwing up and plus, I had gained some weight. I cut all ties with Stella 'cause I just could not face her. I felt like I betrayed our friendship. I finally went to the doctor and he told me I was pregnant with Junior. Cappo was mad, but he also wanted a son, so he raised Junior as his own."

"So, Ms. Tanya, you're telling me my father is a fucking rapist?" Mex yelled. Everyone in the room was heated. It was so tense in the room it felt like we all wanted to explode.

"Mrs. Stella, how do you feel about this?" I asked her.

"Tanya and I have been through so much through the years, shit doesn't even phase me, but the fact that this nigga did this to my best friend and took her away, hurt my heart. Friendship is something you cherish and when you got a friend that you know will have your back through heaven or hell, you don't want to lose that. When I lost Tanya, my world crumbled, but that will never happen again. I have nothing for Sambo, I'm DONE!"

SAMBO

I had heard that my son had a set of twins, but I didn't care about that at the moment. My focus was on money and killing that nigga, Cappo. I know my mind should be focused on putting my family together, but I couldn't do it. I was so mad about Tanya having my seed, then that nigga Cappo named him a Jr. I know that I forced her to have sex, but I wanted her some kind of bad and I knew she would never gave it to me willingly, so I took it. I didn't think I would get a seed out of it though.

Now Stella knew the truth and shit was gone to hell. She wanted a divorce and shit, but I wasn't going to give that to her. Stella belonged to me. I couldn't see her with another man; that would break a nigga for real. But, I remember the lyrics to an R. Kelly song that said, *"when a woman's fed up, there ain't nothing you can do about it."* I knew she was fed up. I had been a dog for so long, but I didn't think she would ever leave me. I would kill any nigga that would step to her. The fact alone that she had moved out and got her own, fucked me up, but I was just giving her time to heal. I know she will be back I'm all she knows.

Niggas in the street knew that she was my woman and they knew what I was capable of, so I knew she wasn't getting with no one local. My ace, Killer had just called me to let know what went down in Cuba with that nigga Cappo. I wished I was there, that nigga would be six feet under right now. I hated that nigga that badly, I would kill his whole family, even my own damn son if I had to. Both of them could get it, if it meant nothing would come back to haunt me. But for some reason I knew Mex had my back, regardless of the situation. He is my flesh and blood and raised by me, so I knew he would ride for his pops when times got hard. I was feeling real nice right now. I had a chick on her knees sucking my dick so good it was crazy. I've received head from all the chicks in the hood, but this young chick, Cha was the truth.

STAR

Tasi thought I had left her ass alone. Nah, I was just sitting back waiting for the right time to get her back. I couldn't get close to Tone, so I got the next best thing, his pops. I was playing my position to get that nigga right where I wanted him. Cha and I came up with a plan to get them niggas. Cha got with Sambo because she was in love with Mex, and could not have him, so she snatched the daddy up. We had the determination to get what belonged to us, and Tasi belonged to me and Mex belonged to Cha. Before everything is said and done, Tasi will be mine and Lyana is going to be miserable.

I could see myself with Killer, but that wasn't my mission. He was a good guy and I really hated to dog him, because he was really feeling a bitch. I just loved Tasi's pussy that much, I would go through anything just to get my girl back. Killer had just walked into the hotel room. We had just left Cuba three weeks ago and now we were in Jamaica. A girl could get use to stuff like this. He had just bought me a dress, when he came in with an Armani suit on, asking was I ready to have dinner with him. I was daydreaming about Tasi so much, I had forgotten about the dinner plans. I got up, took my shower, and off we went to the restaurant. The limo driver dropped us of at an expensive Jamaican spot. I couldn't tell you the name because I was tipsy off the mix I had.

We entered the restaurant and it was the most beautiful thing I had ever seen in my life. Killer helped me to my seat as the waiter came out and opened up some Champagne. I thought, *Champagne, what's the occasion?* He looked at me and said, "Baby, I want you more than you will ever know. I need you in my life forever." Help pulled out a twelve-carat ring and said, "Star, will you be my wife?" *Damn, I done went too far with this shit*, I thought to myself, before everything went black.

TONE

The shit Mex had told me some weeks back about my Godfather, had mentally fucked a nigga up. I looked up to this man all my childhood and to find out what he did to Mrs. Tanya, had me wanting to have nothing to do with him. I couldn't do that because he was like another father to me. I couldn't stop messing with him because he had made me what I am today, him and my dad. I had to wonder if my dad had anything to do with it because regardless, they were family. Although I had to deal with them, it didn't mean I had to forgive them. I had been trying to get with my pops for some weeks now, and couldn't. I wonder what that was about. I know sometimes he would be laid up in some pussy, but this shit was different. I had to talk to this nigga to see what was going on.

I picked up the phone and dialed his number. He picked on the second ring and I began to speak.

"Dang OG, you don't love your son no more? I've been calling you for weeks, shit could have been crazy in the streets and I couldn't get a hold of you."

"I know you straight, I raised you little nigga, only the strong survive. But what's on your mind Lil Killer, talk to me?" he said. I cleared my throat and told him what went on with Mrs. Tanya and Uncle Sambo. My daddy was quiet and I knew what I had told him, fucked him up. I could hear some sniffles on the phone, but I wouldn't call him on it. I felt my dad didn't have nothing to do with what happened. I could tell by his reaction to the news.

"Damn, what the fuck was Sambo thinking? I don't care what goes on, no woman needs to be raped," my pops said. I can tell he's more hurt than anything and the fact that his ace held that information from him, had him thinking crazy shit. He said, "I love you Tone, be safe, and I will call you when I get back."

"Get back? Where are you?" He told me he was in Jamaica with his girl, and would tell me about it when he returned, then hung up. My dad got an ole lady, this got to be a joke, but hey, whatever floats his boat.

MEX

I've been in my own zone. I can't lie, my mind was in a million places right now. I was mad, but being home with my family made me feel so much better. My babies were growing up so fast, and to watch your kids grow was a blessing. My dad raised me to be a man, and to find out he raped someone, had me messed up.

Even though my brother was a product of rape, he was just happy he knew the truth. I could not deal with the look on my mother and sister's faces. I know he broke their hearts to the point it could not be repaired. I knew my mom meant business when her and my sister moved out of my dad's house. She said she was done and her actions proved it. My girl wanted no parts of my dad, and I really couldn't knock her. I mean, she is entitled to her own opinion.

I couldn't understand why my dad hasn't attempted to call or anything. It was like he didn't even care. I couldn't shake the feeling that he needed me. I knew I needed to talk to him to see where his head was at, but I also knew no one would understand my position. I couldn't even talk to Lyana about it, because I knew she would cuss my ass out, and I didn't want those kinds of problems right now. I'm just going to go riding and call this nigga to see what's on his mind.

"Lyana, I'm going out for a while baby, I'll be back later," I yelled to her. She said okay and I headed out to my truck. I rode around for thirty minutes and checked on a few of my traps, before calling my old man. He picked up on the third ring.

As soon as he picked up, he said, "I need to see you, meet me at the park on the East side behind the school," and he hung up. I made my way to the park. It took me a little over twenty minutes to get there. I pulled up and saw my pops talking to some little thots. One tried to holler at me but I wasn't feeling that shit. I had my piece on me because I didn't know what kind of shit this nigga might be on.

He walked up to me and said, "I know you need answers and I'm here to give them to you. I wish your sister were here so I could talk to both of y'all. I was young and dumb and I messed up big time. I messed up a good friendship and broke up a good friendship. I just wanted Tanya so badly; her body was the truth. I knew she would not give it to me because she is loyal to that nigga. I'm a street king, I wasn't used to the word no. If I wanted it, I got it, end of story.

Tanya didn't budge. I had made so many passes at her, but she paid me no attention at all, so I just took what I wanted. I made a mistake and got a son out of it that I don't even know." I had to look at that nigga. He was talking like he had a justifiable cause for raping someone because he is a street king.

"Dad, loyalty is everything, you taught me that, but you were living a lie my whole childhood. I came to hear what you had to say, but really I don't want to hear any more. I love you Dad, but I got to have time to get over this one."

"Look son, I'm sorry. I wish I could take it back, but I can't."

"Whatever Pops," I said and walked away. I felt hurt and relieved. Hurt because he thought his street creditably gave him the right to rape women. Relieved that he told me himself. At the end of the day, he was still my pops, but this whole situation puts me in an odd place.

LYANA

My life is a roller-coaster ride, like really, but being a mother has to be the best ever. The shit my mom told me about Sambo, I knew then I could never let him come near my kids. My children will never know their grandfather, the rapist. My mom is one tough cookie, and I applaud my dad for taking on the responsibility of another man's child. I try to stay out of the street life, but my man was in the streets so I heard things. One thing that ticked me off the most was the fact my dad had my man's stash spots robbed. How could he do that? I don't get the whole street situation, but there are some lines that you just don't cross. The fact that he never told me and Junior about the situation, had me hot.

My phone had rung and when I answered it, I could hear breathing but no one would say anything. They had called five times already, and I was getting frustrated. I was getting my phone number changed tomorrow.

I was so bored in the house. My babies were asleep and Mex was still out. I called Tasi but I knew she was busy, so I got on my FB page. I haven't been on my page in so long I really had forgotten about it. As I was scrolling down my news feed, something caught my eye. I had to stop and read. It read "Congrats to me!" It was Star's page with a picture of just her hand with this big ass rock on it. I called Tasi again, and this time she picked up.

"Girl, I'm on Facebook and guess what I see? Star done got engaged girl, and the rock is huge."

"I'm glad girl, maybe that nigga can keep her off my pubic hairs," Tasi said, and we both fell out laughing. I asked her what was going with her and she informed me she was the face of Covergirl. I jumped up screaming because that was one of her goals since middle school, and my home girl had achieved her dream. Damn we were some lucky bitches. My babies started crying, so I had to go. I guess my screaming did that. Tasi informed me she was flying in tomorrow. She told me to kiss the babies, we said our goodbyes and hung up.

TASI

I was happy as hell when Yana told me Star was engaged. She was a thorn in my thigh that I no longer had to worry about. I was planning my wedding, set to take place winter 2015. I was trying to give my babies a chance to start walking. I was so happy. Who would have thought I would be the model for Covergirl? That was a dream I made a reality.

Tone had been really messed up behind the Sambo situation. There were times he just wanted to say fuck it, but he had that man mentality, so he continued to go about his hustle. We had found a house in Charlotte that was perfect, but I found some land and opted on building from the ground up. I wanted to be comfortable in my crib, so I did it that way so I could design it like I wanted to.

I was going home tomorrow. I missed everyone, especially my babies. Tone said we had to meet up with his pops tomorrow; he had something he wanted to tell us together. I sure hope it was good news because I was tired of getting bad news like, how much could a woman take.

BUG

I was messed with everything that was going on in the crew; shit was crazy. I have known Sambo since Mex, Tone and I were in middle school. They were older than me. I'm nineteen but very mature for my age. I learned from the old heads so everyone said I had an old soul. My name is Travis "Bug" Johnson, standing at six-feet-one, 215 pounds, with dreads that hung past my ass. I got the name Bug, because everyone would always say I was bugging out, trying to talk knowledge to them. It fit so I really didn't care. It just grew on me.

I'm the only child of my moms and the only son from my dad. He has three girls with his wife of six years. I've been thinking a lot about his disloyal situation. I didn't want to be perfidious, but I wasn't right either. I had been seeing Mex's sister, and I knew once he found out, we would be throwing hands. I wanted to be a man about my shit, so I was going to have a talk with him. Keshena didn't want me to tell him because of the age difference. She had just turned seventeen and I was nineteen. I'm a cool ass nigga though, I just stayed to myself and tended to my business.

The one thing about me was I was trigger-happy. I loved to kill people. I didn't have a problem with offing niggas. I wasn't no serial killer though, I only did what was asked from the crew. I wouldn't hurt a soul unless I was told to, and it really had to be a valid reason.

Key had been calling me all day saying she wasn't feeling well, so I told her to come through my crib and chill. She got to my house and I could tell she was sick to her stomach. I told her I was going to take her to the hospital. I got up and we headed to my Range. As soon as we pulled off, she threw up right in my damn car. I wasn't feeling that shit at all, but I could get the shit cleaned up so it was okay.

We finally made it to the hospital and up to the receptionist's desk. As soon as we got there, Key threw up on the receptionist and they hurried up and took her to the back. They admitted her because she was very dehydrated and had severe acid reflux. The doctor also told us she was pregnant. I wasn't expecting that shit because I thought she told me she was on some form of birth control. I knew Mex was going to kill me, but that was one ass whooping I was willing to take, because Keshena was going to have my baby. I didn't believe in that abortion shit. I was so happy, but I could tell Key wasn't feeling that shit at all.

MEX

It's late and I just got word my little sister was admitted to the hospital. I didn't know what was up, but I was concerned. Going to the emergency room and being released was one thing, but to be admitted is another ball game. I just got back to the crib not too long ago. I went upstairs to check on Lyana and the twins. I told her what was going on, gave her a kiss and left. When I got to the hospital, I saw my mom in the waiting room of the third floor. I remembered this floor, because I was on the same floor two months ago for the birth of my twins. If my baby sister was on this floor that meant she was pregnant, but who was the motherfucker that was doing my damn sister?

I called Tone and he informed me that he and Tasi were due in tomorrow, but when I told him where I was at, he said they were coming in on the next flight. My mom came, gave me a hug and told me that my sister was in room 326, and that she is very dehydrated and has bad acid reflux that is making her constantly throw up. I headed in my sister's room and she was in there by herself. She saw me and she knew I knew something was up, for her to be on this floor. I guess my mom left that information out, because she felt Keshena should tell me.

I took a seat in the chair beside her bed and asked her what's up. Key, that's her nickname, looked up to me and said, "Bro, I know you're mad and disappointed in me, but I'm pregnant." I already knew that part, so I wasn't really tripping.

"I know that Key 'cause you on the Labor and Delivery floor, but what I want to know, is who the fuck nigga is?" I could tell she was scared, so I calmed my voice down a little bit. Keshena is my pride and joy, besides my girl, my mom and my twins. I loved that girl and everyone knew I was overprotective of her. I didn't want my baby sis to be like the girls around the way. My sister wasn't in the streets or anything, but yet and still, here she was seventeen and pregnant. I asked her again who the fuck the nigga was.

She looked at me and said, "Bug." I blew out a sigh of relief. Bug is my nigga and not a street nigga off the street. He is a loyal nigga, but I knew something was up with their actions the night my twins were born. Just then, Bug walked into the room. I knew he wasn't expecting me to be there, but I was. He looked scared as hell because he knew I didn't play about my little sis. Like he knew about me, I knew about him. That nigga was deadly. He could kill your ass while you were having a conversation with him.

"Let me holla at you outside brah," he looked at me and said. We went in the hallway and he began to speak. "Look Mex, I know this shit looks fucked up and I've been wanting to tell you about us, but your sister was scared. I'm still a loyal ass nigga, I just didn't really want to stress you man, you got a lot on your plate right now." He was right, I was dealing with major shit in my life, but I'm glad I know now.

"It's all good my nigga. All I ask is that you love my sister and never break her heart. I don't want my sister to be like these ghetto ass chicks out here. She will finish school and she's going to college, I don't care what no one says about that." I dapped him up, embraced him with a hug, told that nigga I loved him and I was out. Bug was my nigga. I had never really seen him have a girlfriend though, so I knew my sister was safe. But if he hurt her, I wouldn't hesitate to send him to his maker. I kissed my mom goodbye and headed back to the crib to get some rest.

TONE

Our plane had a delay so we still arrived on our original day as planned. Tasi and I went straight to Mex and Lyana's house to get settled. I called and checked on Keshena and she told me she was good. I'm glad she was with my nigga Bug, because any other nigga I probably would have bodied. I was just as overprotective of my little sis as Mex was. I saw my God babies and I was so in love with them. Tasi and I were going to wait until after the wedding to try to have kids. We agreed on it. Even with her success, she wanted a family too.

I was getting myself prepared to meet with my pops today, because he wanted to talk to me and Tasi about somethings. We were meeting him at a little spot on the North side, some upscale restaurant called Molans. We got there and my pops was nowhere to be found. I called him and he said he had to cancel because something came up.

"I wish he would have told us that before I wasted my gas," Tasi said. My pops could be such an ass sometimes. I told Tasi fuck that, the nigga was going to see us because I was going to his house unexpectedly. She was all game, but while we were at the restaurant, she said we might as well eat. I understood because I was hungry as hell, and I didn't eat earlier because I was waiting to meet my dad before I ate.

We sat down and ate, and before you know it, the paparazzi were all over us. We couldn't eat in fucking peace. That's the one thing I hate about my girl living in the spotlight, we never had peace really. Someone was always around lurking. We got up and ran to the car and sped off. "Damn paparazzi that food was getting good too." We fell out laughing. We got to my pop's crib in fifteen minutes. His house wasn't far from the restaurant at all. I knew he was there because his Benz was outside, but there was another car there so I knew he had company.

I rang the doorbell and Marie answered the door. She is my

dad's housekeeper (maid). My dad didn't like to use the word maid. He said that meant slave and Maria is no slave, she is the help. He must have saw me outside because he looked like he rushed to put on some clothes.

"Come on in, y'all have a seat. I want to talk to y'all about something." He began to speak me, when Tasi and I heard movement upstairs, but we paid it no mind. He said, "Son, I think I found the one."

"Found the one what, Pops?" I asked, dumfounded.

"I'm getting married son."

"Huh? Congrats Pops, so who's the lucky lady?"

"Baby, come on down and meet my son and daughter-in-law," my pops yelled up the stairs. Me and Tasi looked to the stairs, and down came Star, with tears in her eyes and a deranged look on her face. Tasi fell out laughing.

"This has got to be a joke, right? Whew Killer, you had me there for a minute. Now really, who is the lady in your life?" My pops looked at her like he didn't know what to say.

He looked at Star and said, "You know my son and daughter-in-law, Star?" Star was just standing in the hallway looking crazy.

She started screaming, "I LOVE YOU TASI AND YOU CHOSE THIS FUCK NIGGA OVER ME!!!! I COULDNT GET TO THAT MOTHERFUCKER, TONE SO I SNAGGED THE DAMN DADDY TO GET TO YOU. NOW NIGGA, IF YOU DONT GIVE ME TASI I'M GOING TO KILL YOUR DAD THEN KILL YOU, NIGGA!" Star had my dad's gun in her hand, waving it back and forth between me and my pops. She was demanding Tasi to come to her but I wouldn't let her. Tasi didn't seem fazed at all. I knew my baby was lethal but I knew she didn't have her piece, but I had my piece on me.

Before I knew it, Star was screaming again. "SO, I GUESS I HAVE TO KILL YOU TOO, BABY. WE COULD BE HAPPY

TASI, CAN'T YOU SEE THAT. YOU SAVED ME AND I'M TRYING TO SAVE YOU TOO, BUT YOU WON'T LET ME SO YOU LEAVE ME NO CHOICE!!!!!" Before I knew it, she let off a shot into my pop's arm and he fell back. She shot at me but missed. She ran out the front door, trying to escape. Tasi came from behind me running and slid, tripping Star as she was heading to the door. She fell right out the door onto the pavement. I ran to the door, while Star was on her stomach, trying to get up to make a run for it. She cocked her gun not even looking at what she was shooting at, she was just busting. I heard Tasi yell and I knew she was hit. I pulled out my gun and dumped two bullets into Star's back.

I hurried up and ran to Tasi. I didn't know where she was hit at, all I saw was blood everywhere. I picked her up bridal style and took her in the house. Maria was shook but she had called the police and ambulance. I was holding my baby, telling her to hold on; I couldn't lose my baby. I did something I haven't done in a while and that was pray. I ask God to save my baby, let her be all right.

The ambulance got there and asked what happened. I told them my baby and pops were shot by a crazy woman. The ambulance was about to take Tasi to the hospital, while the nurse techs were doctoring on my pops, preparing to take him to the hospital as well. I was about to go to get in the ambulance, when the police stopped me.

"I need to ask you some questions, sir," they said. I immediately jumped up in the officer's face.

"You'll ask me later because I'm going to be with my wife," I yelled at them.

The officer said, "I understand, sir, you are angry, but can you at least tell me who shot your wife and father, sir?"

"That bitch on that lawn out there with two holes in her back." I pointed to the grass and the officers looked at me like I was crazy. I went outside to look, and I was in disbelief; that bitch was gone!

LYANA

Mex came in the door crying and was yelling, "Baby, get your stuff and get the kids ready now, we have to get to the hospital." I was scared. I asked what the hell was going on. He looked at me and said, "Killer and Tasi have been shot by Star's crazy ass." I thought I would pass out. I started to panic I had to sit down. Mex came and helped me up.

"Baby, I know you are scared and hurt, but Tasi needs you there and she needs you to be strong right now, while she is weak, baby," Mex said. I heard what he said but I could not move. It was like my feet were stuck to the floor. I didn't even feel when Mex left my side. He had the babies in their car seat at the door, waiting for me. I was in my own zone. All I could think was the worst right now. Mex's voice snapped me out of my thoughts.

"Lyana, get up baby, we got to go." He helped me up and put me in the truck. I still wasn't focused on anything, until I heard my baby girl crying. I finally snapped out of it. I grabbed her, cradled her to hush a little bit, kissed her and put her back in the car sit. The cry that escaped me was that of a roar. I just wanted my best friend to be okay. We got to the hospital and everyone was there. I looked up and saw Tone, with his hands on his head crying, with blood all over his shirt and pants. I lost it. I started screaming for the doctor to tell me something. The guards were coming to tell me to calm down, but I was hurting. The fact that my best friend was in surgery fighting for her life, had me on an all-time high. I was seeing red. I wanted to kill that bitch and anyone associated with her.

The doctor came out and we all stood up. "The family of Ms. Weldon." The doctor had this worried look on his face. "Ms. Weldon was shot three times in the stomach, once in her arm and once in the leg. We removed all the bullets, but one bullet pierced her lung and one hit her kidney, and the last one hit her spinal cord. Because the damage is so severe, it could lead to more extreme complications, so we put her in a medically induced coma. We need to let her body heal from her wounds. Now here's the thing. The damage to the spinal cord is what is bothering me the most. The damage may cause her to have to learn to walk all over again, but right now it's up to her to fight." Tone just broke down literally. Killer walked in and he heard the news. He just hugged his son tightly, as both of them cried. Mex was trying to hold them, but he broke down himself. I had to be the strong one, because if I didn't, it would break the rest of the family.

Tasi's mother took it hardest. The doctor took her down to be treated; her blood pressure was so high she fainted. My mom and Mrs. Stella looked at me and said, "We women got to be strong now, we're all we got and we are the backbone of this family." They were right. We had to be strong because these were really trying times for us.

TASI

I couldn't open my eyes. I have tried day in and day out. I could hear everyone around me. I heard my baby, Tone asking me to wake up and I heard Lyana praying for me to wake up. I heard crying voices of my babies and my mother. I had to open up my eyes because I love them dearly. I tried to open them up again, but I still couldn't do it. I felt like giving up, I was tired. I heard Mex come in and say, "Lyana, I'm going to take the babies to my mom's house, let's let them give their Godmother a kiss before they go." I heard them crying again and felt their touch on my cheeks. I felt a tear on my face and I knew it was Antonio; he was my crybaby. Then the next thing I knew, I could see them.

Everyone was happy and I could see my mother giving God the praise. I looked at Yana with tears in her eyes. I said, "Give me my babies."

She fell out laughing and said, "Here, take them, they've been waiting on your ass to wake up." The babies were in my arm so quiet it was like they were relieved I was okay.

Mex said, "Ain't that something? For the past few weeks they've been so fussy, now they just as quiet as they want to be." My doctor rushed in like he was running a marathon.

"Ms. Weldon, I see you're up, I am so glad to finally meet you." Just then, everyone gave me hugs and kisses and left, saying they would be back later. Tone stayed... that's what I loved about my man, he was there through thick and thin. The doc asked me how I was feeling and I told him fine.

"How long have I been in the hospital?" I asked. He told me I'd been in there for two months. I was shocked because it felt like a week. I missed out on a lot in two months. I had to pee so I was listening to the doctor, but I wanted to go to the bathroom. Tone helped me out of the bed, and as soon as my feet hit the floor, I fell. The doctor and Tone helped me back up. I couldn't walk. That shit was so unreal to me, how I couldn't step one foot in front of the other.

The doctor told me how many times I got shot and the severity of my spinal injury. Tone looked at me and said, "Don't worry baby, I got you. We will get you back walking and running in no time. I know you want to run behind A&A." That was the twins' nicknames. The babies were my motivation. Because of them, I was determined to walk again, along with the fact I had to walk down the aisle. I looked up at the TV and the news had a banner on the screen saying, "She's woke!" My fans really loved me.

I knew I had to walk down the runway to show off my curves, so I looked at my doctor and said, "I'm ready to walk again, let's do this.

LYANA

It has been eight months since the shooting of Tasi and Killer, and no one still hasn't heard a thing from that bitch, Star. She was hiding some kind of good. I knew she would come out soon, and I was going to murk her ass. My pops finally reached out to me and wanted me to meet him out of town. He had a business deal in Florida and wanted me to come down so we could talk. Junior was coming too. The babies were going to stay with Mrs. Stella, because Mex had to go out of town as well. He was going to handle some drug meeting.

I had my own office now. I loved my patients and I loved my job. I didn't want to take off, but I told the parents I would be back in three days and gave them the doctor's number that was on call. I was meeting Junior at the airport so we could leave, and of course, he was late as usual. He was running into the airport to catch the flight. It was a snowstorm coming in, to North Carolina, so I was happy to get some sun in Florida. We got on the plane and were off.

I was so happy to have a mini vacation. I needed one. I had been so stressed in the last few months it was crazy. I was helping Tasi with her rehabilitation and she was doing great. She was walking, but not as good as she wanted to be, but she was doing it. We got off the plane and went to the rental my dad had got us. We were staying in Miami. I liked it here; it was nice. We went to our hotel, where Junior had his own room and he was happy, because all he kept talking about was going to look for him some honeys. I looked at that boy like he was crazy. He always thought of butt and girls. I called my pops and told him that we were here. He said enjoy the day and that he was going to get with us tomorrow. I was really tired, so I just wanted to sleep because I haven't had a good night's sleep since I had the babies. So, I laid there until I drifted off to sleep.

MEX

I got a call from my dad telling we had a major shipment in, and I needed to take care of it. I had to go to Florida. At first it was Texas, but the connect changed where we would meet. I knew this was major because I was meeting Martez Deiago, head of the Warlord Mafia. My crew and I went. I didn't want Tone to be here because Tasi needed him, but Tasi insisted he go. My meeting wasn't until tomorrow, so I was going to enjoy myself. I knew my baby was in Miami, so I called her to tell her things had changed. She didn't pick up and I knew she was probably resting, because the babies always kept her up. I needed to rest up, too, but I didn't want to be a party pooper, so I headed out with my boys.

We went to this club on Miami Boulevard. The club was jumping. It had three dance floors and two ice bars. I really needed this. Me and the boys caught up with each other's lives. Bug told me my sister was having a boy, and I was happy. A little knucklehead I could boss around; better yet, Lil Tone, my mini-me could do that. Los told us him and his wife were renewing their vows, and was doing a big wedding and wanted everyone in it.

The first one they had was a courthouse wedding, because they didn't have the money and Christy was pregnant with their second child. I was all game. That makes two weddings soon, Tone and Tasi and now Los and Christy. I'm feeling the marriage vibe. Lyana and I were going to get married after the kids grew up a little more. Tone gave us an update on Tasi, telling us she was walking now. I already knew that because Yana kept me informed on everything. I was feeling the vibe, good music, good friendship, and good family, what more could a person ask for.

STAR

I been in hiding since that shit went down at Killer's house. I told that motherfucker I wasn't ready to meet his fucking son and Tasi's bitch ass. That motherfucker messed up my plans to get Tasi back, and like I thought, that shit wasn't going to be easy. The last thing I wanted to do was to hurt Tasi, but the bitch would not listen when I told her ass to come to me. Call me crazy, but the fact that bitch wouldn't come, made me want her ass more. I loved a challenge, even if it was going to get me killed. While Killer was entertaining Tone and Tasi, I was upstairs planning shit because I knew if I needed back up, Cha would have my back. I called her and told her to be on standby in case I needed her, and I did.

What people didn't know was that Cha was a Registered Nurse, so when that punk ass nigga shot me, I used all of my energy to get the hell out of dodge, with every intent on getting to Cha. I got in my car and sped the hell out of there, while that nigga was carrying Tasi in the house. I wasn't trying to hit her, but I knew he was coming for me, and busting my gun was a distraction. I headed to Cha's house full speed, because I was losing a lot of blood. I made it there and Cha helped me out of the car. I parked in her garage, so when I went in, she closed it and no one saw me go in. It's been damn near half a year, and I was ready for revenge. I was going to get Tasi, but this time I would have the upper hand in the situation. As for that fuck nigga, Tone, I was going to put that nigga six feet under.

LYANA

I woke up the next morning still tired, but that sleep was the truth, I needed it. It felt so different not waking up, hearing my kids, or getting up through the middle of the night. I got up and checked my phone. I had two texts from Mex saying his plans had changed and he was here in Miami. That was good, that meant me and him could have some alone time without the kids. I texted him letting him know that I would hit him up after I met my dad. I headed to the bathroom to take a shower and brush my teeth. I got myself together, put my hair in a messy ponytail, and called my brother to see where he was at. He picked up on the second ring sounding like he had a hangover.

"Junior, where you at?" I yelled.

"Damn, I must have been fucked up last night, I got three bad bitches in the bed with me." I told him he needed to slow his ass down before he caught something. "I got this sis, I stay having the plastic at all times," he laughed.

"Whatever nigga, we got to meet pops in a few so you better get ready," I replied. He told me he had to get the girls up out of there and he would be to my room in an hour. I said okay and hung up. My stomach started doing flips, so I knew I was hungry. I called room service and ordered turkey bacon, eggs grits, grapes, toast and orange juice. As soon as my food arrived, my brother bounced his ass in my room, trying to eat up my food. I said, "Nah player, you had better order your own." He told me we could share, and I was being stingy. I gave in and let him eat some of my food. My phone started ringing; it was my pops telling us to meet him at some warehouse downtown. I was like why a warehouse when we're supposed to be talking about us as a family. He said he had to take care of something. I said okay, but I had a bad feeling about this shit.

KILLER

I came to Miami to handle business with Sambo. He told Mex and the crew to come also, but he didn't let them know that he was here too. Ever since that shit happened with that dizzy bitch, Star, I had changed a lot. I haven't really had a word with Sambo, since I heard the fuck shit he had did to Tanya, and now that we were here face-to-face, I had to address the issue. We are like brothers and for him to keep that shit from me, hurt me.

"Sambo, what the hell man, I thought we were better than that? Why didn't you tell me about the shit that went down between you and Tanya? Better yet, my loyalty to you is real, but you had me believing that Cappo left because he wanted out of the family and thought he could do better than us my nigga. I feel that the shit is fucked, brah. Stella's best friend? Man, I know you knew better than that shit."

Sambo said, "Fuck that bitch Tanya, man, she got what she deserved my nigga. I wanted the bitch but she was *Ms. Goody Two Shoes*. She didn't want to give it to me because she wanted to be loyal to that fuck nigga. You know I don't take rejection well, so I gave her the business. I didn't know I was going to get a kid outta the shit, though. If I had known that, I would have worn a rubber," he said and started laughing. I had to brace myself because I had lost respect for my ace.

"Brah, I go out my way for you. I will steal, kill, rob, and cut a motherfucker for you, Sambo. That shit you did was messed up and you know it. You can have any female you want, and you went for your boy's wife. That shit doesn't sit well with me brah. Not too long ago, I was about to kill Cappo for a reason that I didn't even know, but my loyalty was to you. I was ready to off that nigga. But this is all your fault, all this shit brah, because you can't accept rejection. I would never do you like that brah, never, and you kept that shit a secret for years brah, for years! I had all this hatred for Cappo for something he had every right to be mad at, he had every right to!" I was heated with Sambo. I could really kill him. He was letting his status in the streets take over him and that's something I would never do. I kept my street life and personal life separate.

The nigga had me wondering about my love, Tisha. She left when Tone was two, without even a goodbye or a letter explaining the reason she left. I turned to him looked him dead in the eye and asked, "Have you ever did that fuck shit to me, brah?" His reply was he didn't want to talk anymore.

"Killer, you overstepped your boundaries, so I think you better step the fuck back my nigga." By now, I was ready to off that nigga, bro or not. If he doesn't come with a response to my question, I knew he had done some fucked shit. I asked him again.

"Sambo, look at me nigga when I'm talking to you! Did you fuck, or should I say rape, Tisha?"

He shook his head and said, "Nigga, Tisha was mine first, so it was only right if I tapped the pussy."

He started running and busting his gun the same time, I started busting mine. I was trying to off that nigga, but I had tears in my eyes and missed my mark. That nigga dipped on me somewhere, but I knew one thing for certain, Sambo was now my fucking enemy. I had to find Tisha ASAP. The story Sambo told me was a lie. He told me he saw Tisha the night she left with a man, and she asked him not to tell me because she didn't want to hurt me.

I called Tone and told him to pull out from doing shit with the crew. I don't have anything against my Godson at all, but I didn't trust Sambo now, and I didn't want my son in the mix of things. I needed to make peace, because I could not hate a man that wanted to protect his family, and that was what Cappo was trying to do. I called the last number I had for Cappo. I needed us to call a truce because I didn't really have beef with that man. I just hope and pray he would hear what I had to say.

CAPPO

I was just about to go handle some business and meet my kids, when I got a phone call. I looked at the number, it looked so familiar to me, so I answered the phone. I heard a deep voice and knew who it was, Killer, breathing hard on the other end.

"Cappo, I know you're there, I can hear you breathing. Don't hang up, listen to me for a minute." I pulled the phone away from my ear and wanted to hang up, but something told me to listen to what he had to say. He began to speak.

"First off, let me apologize for what happened in Cuba. If I knew what I know now, I would have never came to you that way. We were close, but you know that Sambo was my ace, so I would ride for him. I never knew why you left the family. I didn't know when I was in Cuba, I found out after that. You have every right to off that nigga, he ain't right. I used to love that nigga, but he had me blindsided. Let me just say what he did to you, he did to me. I know your pain brah, honestly I do. I'm so hurt right now, that nigga fucked a nigga's heart up for real. I just wanted to call you to let you know I'm a man about my shit. I apologize and I have no beef with you.

Sambo is dead to me now so whatever happens, I have no parts in the matter."

I knew it took some heart for a real nigga like Killer to call and apologize. I knew that shit came from the heart. I told him we were good and he would always be my brother. I told him I would call him soon so we could meet, and hung up the phone. The truth of the matter is if he wouldn't have called me, if I would have seen him in streets, I would have thought he was still the enemy. I would have tried to kill that nigga. I had to get to this warehouse to handle some business, and then chill with my kids.

MEX

My night was all love; hanging with the boys was crazy. Tone just called me and told me to come to his room now! I didn't know what the hell was going on but I went to his room to find out. I opened the room door and Tone was on the edge of the bed, with his head down. I said, "What's up Tone, what's going on brah?" When he looked up, I could tell something was wrong.

He said, "Brah, I don't know what's going on, but my dad told me to pull out on this meeting, brah." I asked him did he tell him why he needed to pull out, and he said no, he just told him to pull out.

"You might need to call Uncle Sambo to see what's going on, brah." I called my pops and he picked up.

"Pops, is everything okay? Killer told Tone to pull out, what's up?" He said everything was still a go.

"I don't want Tone to be there, he needs to be home with Tasi. I will be there with you though. I will meet you and the crew on Sunset Boulevard in an hour."

"Brah, whew, you had me scared for a minute there. Pops said he pulled you out 'cause you need to be at home with Tasi man. He was just looking out for you, brah."

Tone said, "I don't think so brah, you should have heard my dad. Something is up and I have a bad feeling about this meeting, Mex. Something is telling me it's not going to end good. Think about it brah, we doing business with the fucking mob. You know they don't play brah," Tone said.

"I will be fine brah, you know how I move nigga." I dapped him up and left out the door. The shit he was saying was fucking with me hard, but I had to focus. My crew and I got ready to go to Sunset Boulevard. We had an assortment of guns just in case something was to pop off. We jumped in the truck and headed out to this meeting. My dad said he was going to meet us there, so I was praying he would be there. I was looking forward to spending a night with my girl. I was sexually frustrated and needed Lyana's pussy bad.

CAPPO

I was ready to get down to business. I had my kids outside because I didn't think this would take long at all. I was meeting a Mafia connect. They wanted the Cuban pure uncut cocaine and I had the best, so they reached out to Papi, who in turn reached out to me. He wanted me to come to this meeting because he didn't want to leave Cuba. I never came alone though. I had a couple of loyal niggas on my team that I loved like brothers, and I would never betray them and vice versa. We had a bond, not like that shit Sambo faked out. Our shit was solid.

I had Cash, Blaze, Tron, Boss, Trap and Dungeon, that was my crew and they couldn't be fucked with. They trained my girls, that's why they were lethal. I had the best of the best. We lived by the code "One for all and all for one." I trusted these niggas with my life and they trusted me with theirs.

I was waiting for these mafia niggas and they weren't even here yet. I mean, who sets up a meeting and be late. This ain't no factory office meeting where niggas come in late, this is serious money we talking about, and drugs. I was giving these niggas a couple of minutes then I was out. I saw a limo pull up, along with five Lincoln Navigators. Those niggas got out like they were ready for war. I didn't need all the men around me because my crew was trained to go. One gun, eight shots added up to twenty kills in my book, so if they thought they were getting a nigga scared, they were sadly mistaken. I don't roll like that, never have and never will.

I saw this short man come in with an umbrella. I was guessing that this man was Mr. Martinez. When he got to me, he said, "I'm guessing you are Cappo?"

"You are right Mr. Martinez. I need to get this ball rolling 'cause I've been waiting for you for you about fifteen minutes, and I don't like to wait, time is money Mr. Martinez."

"I do understand Mr. Cappo, but we still have to wait. I have another investor on this deal and he ain't here yet." I looked at him funny because I knew nothing about this. I asked why I wasn't informed of this.

"I don't play with my money, Mr. Martinez, and if I feel like you're playing, we can dead this shit right now." I heard his men cock their guns and my crew did the same.

Martinez said, "I can assure you I won't waste your time Cappo. I just want to do all business at one time; but, my patience is running thin with the other guy. I'm going to give him a minute if that's okay with you, Mr. Cappo?" I agreed, but I could feel something was off.

LYANA

My dad was in this warehouse with these mafia guys. I saw them get out and they were deep. Me and my brother peeped game though. We saw sharp shooters and knew something was up, so my brother and I got out with our guns on deck, just in case some shit popped off. I looked through the window and saw my pops on one side of the table, and the Italian looking motherfucker was on the other side waiting. I don't know what they were waiting for, but I knew something wasn't right with what I was seeing.

I saw Junior going on top of the building, creeping up behind one of the sharp shooters. I was going to the other side to get the other one. I snuck up behind the man. He was looking through the lens of the gun and didn't even notice me. I stood behind him and popped his neck. We had two more to do. The other one, I really didn't want to walk across the roof for, so I killed him with my silencer attached, head shot to the dome. My dad always taught us kill the sharp shooter first cause they always have the best aim. Now Junior and I were going down to the side of the entrance to wait to see what was going on.

MEX

My dad was hardheaded. He acted like he could not wait for me and my crew, and we were like ten minutes out. I told him this on the phone, but he was yelling at me.

He said, "Mex, I told you to be here and you running late. I had these people waiting for me for like five minutes. Do you know I'm dealing with the fucking mafia Mex, the fucking Mafia? I can't have my face bad Mex, if I do, they probably would not do business with me again. I need that connect right now. I need to expand more, I need to have my name known all over, do you understand Mex?" I was listening to my pops, but he was sounding real crazy right now.

I didn't know what the hell he was on, but he was acting crazy. I looked at the crew and they were looking like, *what the fuck is going on with pops*. I could not even answer that question.

He yelled, "Look, I'm going in, y'all get here when y'all get here. I can't have y'all slow motherfuckers messing my plans up. If y'all keep fucking up, I won't be messing with y'all period. I'm out, hurry the fuck up Mex," and he hung up on me. I was getting there but damn, I could kill my crew in the process. The traffic was hectic, but I was going to be there for my pops.

LYANA

Junior and I were at the back door, waiting to see if some shit was going to pop off. I could see the Italian man getting real impatient.

He screamed, "All y'all fucking Americans don't know how to handle fucking business. Either you are fucking late or fucking dead. I hate dealing with y'all mutha fuckers, y'all can't seem to do a damn thing right! But y'all fuckers bring me so much fucking money that I can't stop fucking with y'all."

Just then, I heard tires screeching from a car or truck. I saw a man run in the warehouse trying to explain himself why he was late.

The Italian man said, "Now you're here you mutha fucker. I tell you this Mr. Sambo, you will never in your fucking life have to worry about doing business with me again."

When I heard the name Sambo, I knew it was about to be some shit, because my pops had been trying to get close to him for years, and now they were in the same building. Before the thought was completely formulated in my head, shots were fired from every direction. When the smoke was clear, everyone was gone. Junior went to check around the building to see if he could find my dad. I saw a body in the middle of the floor.

I went up to the body on the floor with my gun drawn, because I didn't know what else could pop off. As soon as got to the body, I heard voices. I turned the body over with my foot, as the voices got closer. I saw that it was Sambo. I heard a voice that scared the shit out of me. It was Mex and he looked at me with a cold ass stare.

"Hey Yana, you killed my fucking pops, yo?" Before I could get the words out to say NO, my whole world went black.

Text ROYALTY to 42828 to get a

notification when more from this

author comes out!

More coming soon from

ROYALTY PUBLISHING HOUSE!

Text ROYALTY to 42828 to get a

notification when they come out!

If you would like to join our team, submit the first 3 -4 chapters of your completed manuscript to submissions@royaltypublishinghouse.com

CPSIA information can be obtained at www.ICGtesting.com
Printed in the USA
LVOW07s1454221015

459337LV00018B/957/P